What a terrific book tha
storm and find a lasting at
Robert Boyd Delano's w
genius, the late Eugenia Pr.
subplot throughout this masterful book has been woven together into fine tapestry.

On page after page, the unique Post-World War II background and the characters spring to life, readily identifiable. It is an immensely and intensely enjoyable book.

—Jimmy and Roxanne Clanton
Houston, Texas
Rock 'n Roll Teen Idol ("Just a Dream" and "Venus in Blue Jeans"); authors of the book, *Hardcore Health,* and internationally-syndicated eColumnists on MyBestYears.com

I literally couldn't put the book down!

As a young man driving a tractor on the "Sledge Place" that became part of our own farm, I often wondered about the family by that name and whatever happened to the young people who used to live there when they were my age?

Imagine my delight, nearly a half-century later, to pick up this historical novel, *The Happy Immortals,* written by Robert Boyd Delano, a grandson of the Sledges who homesteaded that same farmland.

R.B. had also grown up on a nearby farm. In fact, I discovered that Bob, as he is known to friends, actually lived with my great-grandparents for a couple of years during the late-1930s so he could attend Guymon High School. It's definitely a small world, isn't it?

Though I began reading this page-turner while in the nation's capital, I was instantly transported back to my homeland. This poignant Tom Bristow love story is a nostalgic flashback of growing up on an Oklahoma Panhandle wheat farm near Guymon, and I identified so much with the scenes R. B. described and the story he told.

The values and experiences of this hard-working, tough-love father and his pressured son are intertwined with Tom's struggles to find true love and happiness. Tom's pursuit of a forbidden love and his stubborn medical career choice shatter Benjamin Bristow's dreams for him and add a deeper dimension to this story.

—Larry A. Quinn
Washington , DC
Career Communicator; former Guymon radio station announcer

The Happy Immortals reaches out of the 1940s and pulls the reader into that decade's landscape, language, values and visual details, courtesy of a writer who saw it all and remembered it vividly. We can be grateful Robert Delano persisted to pen this novel.
—Ann DeFrange
Oklahoma City, Oklahoma
Columnist, *The Oklahoman*

The realistic descriptions of Oklahoma Panhandle agriculture and scenery added a rich dimension to this well-crafted story. Having grown up in the area, I quickly remembered various landmarks as they were introduced and explained throughout the book. These locations, described in colorful detail, supplied valuable context and provided an excellent setting to the story. I thoroughly enjoyed this uplifting tale of one man's quest for that which is truly important in life.
—Garvin W. Quinn, Ph.D.
Knoxville, Tennessee
Agricultural Communicator
and Educator

Robert Boyd Delano has authored a very interesting read with *The Happy Immortals*. The storyline is excellent. His style of writing is captivating and enjoyable.

As a son of the Oklahoma Panhandle, I was thrilled to have my heart turned toward home by Robert's novel. His descriptions of the Guymon area and the dynamics of living in that unique "No Man's Land" region were incredibly accurate and poignant. Also, as one born and raised in the setting of the novel, I can affirm the lifelong connection to the land, no matter where you reside—its landscape and people remain in your heart forever.

In so many ways, I saw myself in the character of Tom Bristow. I would definitely recommend *The Happy Immortals* for enjoyable reading!
—Dr. Larry C. Taylor
Colorado Springs, Colorado
Church Adminstrator

The Happy Immortals

Robert Boyd Delano

The Happy Immortals

ISBN-13: 8-0-9790312-0-5
ISBN-10: 0-9790312-0-6

© 2007 by Prairie Hill Press and Robert Boyd Delano

PO Box 270398
Flower Mound, TX 75027
www.prairiehillpress.com

Typesetting and layout by Ken Fraser

Printed in the United States of America
1 2 3 4 5 6 7 8 9 10 11 12 PHP 15 14 13 12 11 10 09 08 07 06

This is a work of fiction. While actual geographical locales are used for background, the names, characters and incidents are either the product of the author's imagination or are used fictitiously, and any resemblance to actual persons—living or dead—or events is entirely coincidental.

No part of this book may be reproduced or transmitted in any form or by any means, electronic or mechanical—including photocopying, recording, or by any information storage or retrieval system—without permission in writing from the publisher. Please direct all inquiries to admin@prairiehillpress.com.

This book is dedicated to...

My parents, Chance and Eula Delano, hardy Oklahoma Panhandle immortals, whose faith endured those treacherous Dust Bowl days, and whose iron-willed legacy continues to flourish through the generations that have followed,

My wife Margie, without whom this book and my life would have little meaning,

And all those who seek happiness and find joy.

1

Tom removed his fashionable gray fedora and pressed his face against the passenger train's window, holding his breath to avoid steaming up the glass and obstructing his view. Finally, Anna's taut, straining figure caught his eye as the train's brakes continued scraping against the wheels and the clacking sounds grew farther apart. He could see her brown eyes searching each window as they passed her, little lines of apprehension wrinkling her brow beneath a narrow-brimmed rain hat. She stood a little apart from a knot of Guymon's citizenry who looked to be as much a part of the scenery as the depot.

Anna saw him now as his car pulled even with her. Apprehension melted into radiance, and she started running alongside to keep pace with him. The hissing and bell-ringing of the train swallowed up the words her lips were forming, but she kept going, her baggy raincoat billowing out behind her as she sloshed through one puddle after another. Her eyes never left Tom's as she ran, and he shivered at the thought of her running into something or getting her legs tangled in her raincoat and being thrown into the train's wheels.

The train finally came to a stop and Tom was the first passenger down the steps.

"Anna, you shouldn't be out in this rain," he scolded

when their first long, warm kiss had ended. He had felt her chin quivering against his face but her lips were the same sweet yielding lips that he had craved intermittently now for…for how long? Since their junior year in high school when her family moved to Guymon? Could it be over ten years? Could it be over eight years since they walked down the aisle together in the high school auditorium, class of 1940, and received their signed, symbolic sheepskins?

    She was the same Anna, always wearing her beauty like an old coat, as though it belonged to her, as though she had not manufactured it but had accepted it, loved it and was comfortable in it. Even the tiny beauty mark on the left side of her face was worn with charm like most women wear jewelry.

    "I haven't been here long—I'm not wet," she said, linking her hand in the crook of his arm. Tom looked at the dark, water-sogged shoulders of her raincoat and smiled at her effort to please him. She looked admirably at him—regally tall, imperially slender, impeccably dressed, and with the dreamiest cobalt-blue eyes and dark, wavy brown hair.

    "Let's get in out of the rain where we can talk," he said, reaching up and pushing his soft felt hat tighter on his head as they leaned against the wind-swept showers.

    A brand new 1949 Ford coupe splashed past, glistening in the rain as windshield wipers valiantly tried to stay up with the downpour. The couple moved away from the railroad terminal. They walked quickly along the rain-glistened red brick of the depot yard and a half-block down Guymon's Main Street until they came to a dingy-fronted café known as the Silver Grill. It held its place comfortably and securely in a two block row of business buildings that had faced each other across Main Street in languid stability since Tom could remember. The same stores had always been there, waiting in their county-seat confidence for him, like Anna, each time he returned to the Oklahoma Panhandle.

Tom had once looked upon Guymon as a metropolis—the center of the universe—but that was long before he had graduated from GHS, class of 1940, before he headed to Oklahoma University, before he had entered the U.S. Army the day after graduation from OU, before he had known Okinawa in the final year of World War II, and before attending the Saint Louis University School of Medicine.

Coincidently, Tom had decided that his father's beloved Hawk Ranch was not the hub of the world either.

"Two coffees," Tom said to the stubby little waitress. It was two o'clock in the afternoon and all the booths were empty except the one in which he and Anna sat. A wiry man with Ben Franklin spectacles and a sallow-complexion sat behind the cash register reading a copy of the *Panhandle News-Herald*. He had glanced at them briefly when they entered, but seemed indifferent to them as customers.

"Oh, it just occurred to me that you might like to have something besides coffee. You probably haven't had any lunch," Tom said, embarrassed at his thoughtlessness.

"No, coffee's fine. I had lunch with mother before I came down to meet you." She smiled, studying him as though checking to see if anything about him had changed. She seemed satisfied with her analysis. "Have you eaten anything?"

"Yes, the Rock Island took care of that for me." Tom was thankful for the privacy that the scant patronage inside the Silver Grill afforded. He had been mentally rehearsing what he wanted to say to Anna during the entire train ride from St. Louis.

"I'm so glad you could come out, Tom," Anna's eyes radiated warmth and concern. "I didn't get to see much of you during your brief Christmas weekend. And when you called yesterday and said you were coming, I got so excited I didn't think to ask what the occasion was...not that there has to be one."

She was smiling as she spoke, but a look of curiosity crept into her eyes. "Are you between semesters?"

"Yes, it's between semesters. But that doesn't matter. I would have had to see you and talk to you even if it were in the middle of final exams. An idea has been gnawing at me for a long time, and I've got to tell you about it or I'll rip at the seams."

Tom paused while the bubbly, stubby waitress served steaming coffee in thick ironstone mugs. His legs and back ached from the train ride. He usually slept soundly in a Pullman, but not last night. The clickety-clacks had grown louder with each mile, but not loud enough to shut out the thoughts that crowded in. He couldn't wait to tell Anna his new idea and was excited to see what she would think about it.

The waitress left. Tom spoke quickly, "I wanted to talk to you about it during the Christmas holidays but, like you said, we were never alone. Besides, I wasn't as sure of my plan then as I am now."

Anna set her cup down and leaned forward, curiosity growing in her eyes. "Well, come out with it, don't keep me in suspense."

Tom took a swallow of the black, steaming coffee. It smelled good but the hot edge of the cup stung his lips. He set the cup back on the saucer and said, "It's something we've both wanted for a long time."

Anna smiled, the curiosity turned to excitement. "I know what it is," she said teasingly. "They're going to give you your M.D. a semester early, and then you're going to intern at Guymon Memorial Hospital so you can be near me." She laughed her soft throaty laugh and leaned over close to him, her lips turned up toward him like she was seeking a kiss.

"No. It's better than that. Well, in a way it's better. The overall plan is better. I've worked it out so we can be married right now!"

"Keep talking," she said, raising an eyebrow skeptically, the teasing gone from her voice.

"It'll mean me leaving school." Tom paused and sipped at the still-too-hot coffee, watching Anna's face, hoping to see it light up in a flush of acceptance. Seeing none, he continued hurriedly: "I've never mentioned it before, but medicine is losing its enchantment for me. I liked pre-med and the first year or two afterwards were tolerable, but since then...since then it has been one long stretch of pretense and agony. I can't tell you everything, but things have happened recently to help me see just how I don't want to do this for the rest of my life. I've pretended to like it just to please Dad. You know how crazy he has always been for me to become a doctor."

Tom tested his coffee again and found it slightly more comforting this time. He gulped from the heavy cup, waiting to see what Anna would say. Nothing came. She sat staring at her coffee, twisting the cup back and forth on the saucer. Ill-concealed disappointment now filled her face.

"I can't pretend anymore," Tom said. "I want to do what I want to do—not what Dad wants me to do. I want to be free, to work outside in the fresh air. I'm sick of the smell of medicine, and I'm sick of sickness, cadavers and the hypocrisy of those that take the Hippocratic Oath. I want the fresh air of the Hawk Ranch, and I want to be free to be with you."

"But Tom...you've worked so long for it. It would be such a waste for you to drop medicine now." Anna's eyes reddened as she stared at him, her lips quivering in unbelief. "Besides, we need doctors. Look at Mother lying flat on her back the past few years, wasting away because no one has found a cure for her heart problems."

"That's what I mean, Anna. Can't you see? It's all so useless—so many incurable diseases, so much pain that medicine hasn't begun to touch. Oh, sure—someone will occasionally stumble onto a vaccine, but you knock out one disease and two others will take its place. Medicine primarily consists of passing out pills and with not too much more efficacy than in Hippocrates' time. We just do a better job of selling it now." His voice trailed off unconvincingly as he said all the words he had practiced silently on the railroad train ride to Guymon. Suddenly, the coherent, powerful statements were falling flat, splashing like raindrops on the sidewalk just outside the café window.

"You can't believe that, Tom," Anna said, turning her head to one side in an accusing glance. "Besides, your father would be outraged. He'd simply die!"

Tom looked away from her. The steamy window beside them revealed the curved shadows of more cars and trucks along Main Street. She had hit a nerve and she knew it. She knew how his father had planned and worked for him to become a doctor; how he had required him to forego baseball and even manual labor on the ranch for fear he would knock down some knuckles and make his fingers less dexterous; how he had kept after him year after year to improve his grades and had finally succeeded in getting him accepted into the University of St. Louis Medical School after he returned from serving in the army. She knew how badly Benjamin Bristow wanted the M.D. for his son. Tom knew it even more. Throughout his life, it was an ironclad milepost that loomed on the horizon. His father knew what he wanted for Tom, and Tom had always assumed that it was his destiny, simply because his father said so. Questions, once fleeting shadows, had become mountains.

"So that was it," Tom's thoughts flashed crazily as the words from Anna's mouth tormented him. "I have to give up what I want so my father's wants can be satisfied." For years, Benjamin had put him in a one-way, non-stop rut and there seemed to be no way of escaping.

Suddenly, momentarily, Tom did escape, faraway. Okinawa beckoned him. He saw Higa standing, welcoming him back. She was always available to him, a distant memory he could run to whenever he needed, an emergency antidote that he kept in reserve that no one knew about except himself. Higa was as real as Anna or his father, even though she was separated from him by five thousand miles of Pacific water and a half-decade of trying to put her out of his mind. No one would know how he had tried to forget Higa. But she always came back to him, usually when he least expected her, when he was in the middle of a grueling final examination or, sometimes, at the very moment he was kissing Anna. And now, she was back in his thoughts.

He forced himself back to Guymon, to the present, to the booth where he sat with Anna.

"Maybe you're right," he said, more angrily than he had intended. "Let's forget it now."

He threw a tip on the table and handed a dollar to the old man behind the cash register. While he waited for the change, Anna came up beside him and put her hand on his arm. He felt his muscles tighten and he avoided looking at her so she wouldn't see the anger in his eyes.

Why did she have to be so hide-bound to her ill mother? If it weren't for that, they could have been married years ago. And why did she have to be so contrary now about his determination to give up medicine? It was the only way they could have each other now. Why couldn't she have accepted his plan, not necessarily with enthusiasm, but at least with simple agreement. Instead, she seemed to echo everything his father wanted. She was like the professors at school and like his father.

Responsibility. Self-discipline. What you do now will determine your future. Make good choices or somebody else will have to decide for you. Never sacrifice the future on the altar of the present.

Everything had to be so complex. Suddenly, he wanted to get away, to sort out his ragged thoughts. He didn't really want to hurt her, but...

"I'll see you later," he said, pulling his arm away from her and carefully doffing his fedora. He walked to the door and turned to look at her. He could see the disappointment in her eyes.

"We were expecting you for dinner. Mother and Dad will be..." She stopped after walking halfway to the door biting her lip. Waiting.

"Tell them hello for me," Tom shot back, more brusquely than he really wanted it to sound. "I'll take a rain check on the dinner."

Tom opened the door and stepped out into the drizzling rain. His insides felt empty and sick. He wondered if Anna had stayed behind in the café, and after a half block he turned and looked back toward the Silver Grill; there was no sign of her. He pulled his hat down further on his head and buttoned the top button of his raincoat. He stood, waiting, staring at the front door of the Silver Grill. Finally, a taxi sputtered its way down the street, its noisiness breaking the dull monotony of the rain. The driver, Archie, was a bushy red-headed man with only one arm. Tom had seen him driving Guymon's lone taxi since he could remember. He waived him over to the curb.

"There's a young woman. Anna Taylor. You may know her..."

"Yep, the preacher's daughter. Right?"

"Yes, Dr. Taylor's daughter," Tom answered, bending down so he could talk without shouting. "She's in the Silver Grill. See that she gets home without walking in the rain. He handed the driver a five dollar bill. As Archie started to roll up his window and drive away, Tom yelled as an afterthought, "Give her time to stop by the grocers! She always buys groceries on Saturdays."

Archie stopped his cab momentarily, turning to look at Tom, holding a soggy cigar with two fingers of his only good hand and using the other two fingers on the steering wheel. Then the driver pulled away, drove to the end of Main Street, made a U-turn, and headed back to the Silver Grill. He pulled up to the curb and honked.

Tom moved over behind a neon sign and watched as the driver honked the second time. Maybe she had slipped out of the café without him noticing and was walking home in the rain. He felt better when he saw the door to the grill swing open. Anna walked to the waiting cab. She stood beside the cab for a moment, bending forward, talking to the driver, her hands tucked away in the pockets of her raincoat. Tom kept watching as she straightened up and glanced down the street in his direction before getting into the cab. He had an urge to jump out from behind the sign and run to her, to apologize for his boorish behavior, to ask her forgiveness, to kiss and make up. The moment was gone before he could decide, and the cab with its precious cargo drove out of sight.

Tom was left alone with his blinking, hissing neon sign. The empty, sick feeling within him grew larger. Drops of rain dripped off the brim of his hat. For the first time he realized he was standing next to neon letters that spelled LONNIE'S POOL HALL. Behind the sign, a well-worn door leading into Lonnie's stood slightly ajar. The smell of hamburgers and beer blended comfortably with the sound of men laughing. It was a warm, dry place. He opened the door a little wider and walked in.

"Give me a large draw and a sack of peanuts," Tom said, sitting down on one of the plain wooden stools in front of the bar. His voice sounded curt even to himself, but no one seemed to notice. The bald-headed man behind the bar moved quickly through a well-worn routine of grabbing a mug, setting it under a spigot and watching the yellow body of the beer eat its way up through the sudsy head.

Lonnie's was the same as it had always been. The bald-headed bartender was more of a waiter than a barkeep. A grease-fringed short-order menu above the bar offered the same spaghetti-red, chili-with-beans, chili-plain, ham sandwich, cold-beef sandwich, bean soup and "Today's Special." The prices had changed, though only slightly, since Tom used to come to Lonnie's with other high school chums for a game of eight ball or snooker.

Back then they were too young to buy beer, but occasionally they would manage for an intermediary to get it for them. Then they would sneak the golden, forbidden liquid back to the restroom. Amid rank waves of urine stench and graffiti-covered walls, they splashed it down youthful throats amid raucous and boisterous laughter. The mere thought of those moments brought back the smell—the pungently blended odors of beer and stagnant urine.

It was a strange place for young boys to go, it seemed to Tom now, but back then the place held a magnetic, special attraction. There was something dangerous and alluring about the dank, almost evil, dimly-lit spot that kept them coming back. Perhaps it made them feel superior to slip something by the adults, but he never thought about it that way before.

After a couple more draws from the frothy amber brew, Tom began to feel a sense of satisfaction, a sort of giddy comfort from this sameness that pervaded Lonnie's Pool Hall. Two snooker tables still held their rank at the head of a row of other smaller and less pretentious pool tables. The "reds" and "colors" on the snooker tables made the same merry clacking sounds as the solid and striped balls on the pool tables as they raced over the fuzzy green felt cloth in response to smack after smack of cue sticks. It was a cacophony of striking ivory sounds that filled the room with a percussive symphony, blending perfectly with the Hank Williams' honky-tonk song blaring in the background from the jukebox:

> I got a feelin' called the blues, oh, lawd,
> Since my baby said good-bye
> And I don't know what I'll do
> All I do is sit and sigh, oh, lawd
> That last long day she said good-bye
> Well lawd I thought I would cry
> She'll do me, she'll do you
> She's got that kind of lovin'
> Lawd, I love to hear her when she calls me
> Sweet daddy, such a beautiful dream
> I hate to think it all over
> I've lost my heart it seems
> I've grown so used to you some-how
> Well, I'm nobody's sugar-daddy now
> And I'm lonesome
> I got the lovesick blues.

Tom ordered another large beer and ambled with it and his peanuts back to the second table, distancing himself from the jukebox and its mournful tune. He strained to listen to the clicking cue sticks, the colorful conversations, the clanging pans in the kitchen—anything besides the depressing song.

Something about a man playing snooker at that table made him stop and study him for a moment. He was muscular and his red, pudgy face almost hid two small eyes that peered out at the balls on the table. Except for his massive size, the man looked strikingly familiar.

Then Tom remembered. It was Willie! Tom couldn't remember the guy's last name. When Tom was in high school, Willie had been a skinny, wiry guy. This man had the same crooked teeth, but he was huge. Of course, a decade would change him a lot. Still, it definitely was Willie.

"What was his last name?"

Tom watched him as he crouched to shoot, then as he straightened up and pulled a cigar from his heavy lips. He seemed to enjoy pouring out colorful expletives toward his cue stick and the balls on the table.

"Lusby!" That was it. "Willie Lusby."

Tom tossed the remainder of his peanuts into his mouth and took a long swallow of beer. He had almost forgotten how the foamy head on a beer tickled his lips. It had been a long time, especially under the withering schedule of medical school, since he had drunk any beer. Too long. This was living! He felt care-free, taking another long swallow.

He sat down on a high-legged chair by the table where the red, pudgy faced man was playing.

"Seven ball in the corner, Jennings," the big man said. Grinning cruelly, Willie laid his cigar butt on the edge of the table, "and if I make it I'll have your ass stretched over a barrel."

His small eyes gleamed. Sliding the cue stick back and forth knowingly through his curled fingers several times, he cracked the cue ball into the seven, knocking it into the corner pocket just as he had predicted.

"That gives me the game," the big man said, chalking the score noisily onto the chalkboard.

Jennings had been standing unobtrusively to one side, so quiet that Tom suddenly now realized he was a party to the game. He was average height but almost as slender as the cue stick he leaned on. In fact, the stick seemed to be propping him up as if it were a crutch. His skin was well-tanned, almost leathery. From his clothes and demeanor, Tom judged him to be a farmer or farmer's hired hand who had come into town to enjoy a rainy Saturday afternoon off.

Jennings stood for a moment after the seven ball

thudded into the pocket, his lips quivering as though wanting to say something but unable to get it out. He looked nervously toward the blackboard and the score seemed to drain the color from his face. Finally, without saying a word, he walked over and racked his cue stick and started to leave.

The pudgy faced man stuck a heavy, hairy arm out to bar his way.

"You forget something, plowboy?"

The skinny man looked up at him with a surprising amount of defiance. He said nothing but tried to duck under the heavy arm.

"You ain't getting out of here without paying me, hoss!" The pudgy one grabbed a handful of Jenning's shirt as he spoke.

Jennings still looked a little defiant but his voice was whiney and pleading, "You...you didn't add the score right, Willie. It's a tie and I don't owe you a damned cent. We both got forty-seven."

He pointed at the numbers on the blackboard and Tom could see, quickly adding the figures in his head, that the pudgy-faced man, Willie, had erroneously given himself forty-nine instead of the correct total of forty-seven.

"You're crazier'n hell," Willie shot back, his voice sounding even more cruel. "Pay me the damned fifty we bet fair and square, or I'll wring your skinny neck."

The thin man glanced furtively, desperately around the room, leaning back limply in the shirt that Willie still grasped in his meaty fist. His frightened eyes stopped on Tom.

"You can add, can't you, mister?" he asked plaintively, pointing to the obvious two point error on the blackboard. "What do you say the score is?"

Willie joined the skinny one in staring at Tom, both waiting for him to speak—the skinny one like an accused man waiting for the judge to pronounce his sentence, and the pudgy-faced one much as a prosecuting attorney confident he had already won his case.

Tom got up from his chair and set his beer mug down. For a moment the two faces seemed to consist of four glaring eyeballs.

"Why should I get involved?" he thought quickly. "Let them fight their own battles."

Tom looked at both of the men: "Uh...I haven't been paying much attention."

Deliberately, he turned away from the desperate eyes of the skinny one and started walking toward the front of the pool hall. After a few steps, he stopped and started to explain that he had to have another beer, but the two men weren't looking at him anymore. The pudgy-faced one was shoving the skinny one out the door and into the alley behind the pool hall. Tom didn't know why, but he felt somehow compelled to follow a dozen or so other pool hall patrons who were scurrying outside to see what would happen. Tom slipped out of the back door just in time to see the lanky farmer pull himself up from the foul sogginess of the alley mud. He staggered to his feet and brushed at the mud splattered on his trousers by the fall, mumbling at the same time about the two point error.

Tom noticed that the rain had stopped falling. Still, the alleyway was a sporadic series of muddy pools. The farm hand was standing in the center of one.

"I'm giving you one more chance to pay me the bet, Jennings." Willie's face was a twisted grin of superiority. "You'll pay one way or the other, and it don't make me no never-mind which way it is."

Jennings was still bent forward wiping at the mud on his trousers when the blow landed. It caught him on the side of his thin nose. Tom heard the cartilage snap and saw the blood spurt at the same time. He wouldn't permit himself to look away, not even after the pudgy one picked his victim up and hit him again and again.

Quickly, within moments, the skinny one's desperate eyes were swollen shut and the slim features had become almost unrecognizable. Tom wanted to grab the pudgy one and stop the massacre, but he couldn't bring himself to do it.

Finally, an old man came from inside the pool hall and waded in to stop the one-sided fight. For some reason, the elderly gent didn't seem afraid of Willie at all. The bully quit with surprising willingness, apparently content with his bloody spoils. Willie wiped his blood-stained knuckles victoriously, deliberately, on his jeans, grinned triumphantly at the people in the circle, then stalked back into the pool hall.

Tom stayed behind to help the old man pick Jennings up out of the mud. After a little coaxing, the two men brought the plowboy around enough to get him to his feet.

"Everybody knew he was cheating me," Jennings mumbled between clinched teeth, "but nobody would say so. Everybody knew he was cheating me—everybody!"

The old man went back inside the pool hall. Tom squatted down beside Jennings, forcing himself to stare at the bleeding face. The rain started falling harder than before. Blood from the cowboy's face washed onto the alleyway's mud.

"I'm sorry," Tom said, "I knew he was cheating, too. You were right. I knew."

Tom pulled out a clean white handkerchief and placed it carefully with a practiced hand over the nose to stop the flow of blood. Then he helped him through the alley and to the farm hand's ancient, rust-covered Chevrolet pickup truck.

"I'm truly sorry." Tom tried to keep his voice steady. "I should have helped. I just..."

Impulsively, Tom reached into his back pocket for his leather wallet, pulled out a fifty dollar bill, and jammed it into Jennings' hand.

"Maybe this will help," he said. "Maybe it will help make up a little for what I should have done. Maybe it will help you with…"

Jennings looked at Tom for a moment through swollen eyes, then his eyes that had flickered momentarily with a glimmer of gratefulness turned a steely, hateful, hopeless gray. The farmhand stuck the currency into his would-be benefactor's chest pocket, opened the creaky door to his pickup, and through bloody lips spat out the words, "Take your money, mister, and go buy yourself some damned guts."

2

Tom stood under a Main Street awning, watching the farm hand drive away. He kept seeing the lacerated face and the sound of those defiant words, "Take your money, mister, and go buy yourself some damned guts." He desperately wanted to leave behind the scenes of Willie, Jennings, Lonnie's Pool Hall and the alleyway behind him. The rain was the only diversion, and he tried to concentrate on the large raindrops that rolled down over the edges of the awning above him, then as they splashed ostentatiously against the concrete walk.

Suddenly a lean young man about his own age dashed across the sidewalk in front of him carrying a sack that smelled of fresh-baked bread. His long strides swept him quickly to a red Ford pickup truck which was parked at the curb, less than twenty feet from where Tom stood. A smiling and very pregnant young woman leaned over in the cab of the truck and pushed the door open for him. She took the sack as he sat down and her lips, full and glowing with the tenderness that pregnancy imbues, opened and closed with words Tom could not hear. The way she looked at and talked with the young man spoke volumes. They obviously cherished each other. It reminded Tom of the way Anna looked at him. That only served to heighten the loneliness he already felt.

He almost hated the young man who leaned toward the young woman and kissed her yielding lips. They kissed as though the center of their universe was right there in the cab of their red pickup truck. The couple seemed so blissful and happy.

Why couldn't he and Anna be like that? Why did Anna's mother have to be sick? Why did he have to waste his life away at med school just because of his father's dream? Why couldn't life be easy and simple, as it appeared to be for the kissing couple?

Tom was lost in his thoughts as the truck backed away from the curb, then drove into the rain, leaving unprotected a couple of greasy circles on the red brick pavement. Tom watched as the rain enhanced those droplets with all the vivid colors of the rainbow. He was still staring at the spots on the pavement and became annoyed when a car drove up and parked, obscuring the colorful mixtures of oil and water.

It was a moment or two before he realized it was the battered taxi and its one-armed driver that he had called on for help earlier that afternoon. Tom moved out from under the awning, sprinting the half-dozen steps to the taxi, hoping to avoid the deluge. Quickly, he slid in the front seat beside Archie.

"How long has it been since you've seen a movie?" he asked the driver.

The one-armed man looked startled at the unexpected directness. He rubbed his chin for a moment as he puffed heavily on his cigar. "Been quite a spell, I reckon. I `spose it was *Key Largo* a few months ago with that Bogart fella." He took the cigar out of his mouth. "Why'd you wanna know that?"

Tom reached in his pocket and brought out his billfold. He sifted through an assortment of bills and selected a twenty dollar bill which he held confidently out to the driver.

"Would you rent me your cab for a couple of hours?

You could go in out of the rain and see a movie while I'm gone." Tom could see he was making headway. "I'll take good care of it. I'll treat it just like it was my own." He thumbed through his billfold and, flipping it open so the driver could see, he said, "I've got a driver's license—see?"

The driver seemed convinced of the reasonableness of Tom's proposition and he hopped out, grinning and puffing merrily on his cigar. "It's a deal," he said, handing the keys to Tom. "You got yourself a cab for a couple of hours."

Anna's face showed obvious surprise when Tom knocked at the parsonage. Dr. Taylor was in his study working on the next day's sermon and her mother had been given something to help her sleep, so she was comfortable for the time being. By that time the rain was pouring down again.

Tom pointed to the taxi and asked Anna to go for a drive. "Your chariot awaits," he gestured dramatically, as if his humor could make her forget what had happened at the Silver Grill.

"You pick the rainiest days to come see me, Doctor Bristow," Anna said cheerily, donning her raincoat, slipping her arm in his for the short walk, then sliding into the front seat of the old taxi cab beside him. She had been using the Doctor title on him during her lighter and chiding moments ever since he started medical school.

"Where's our chauffeur?" she asked.

"I gave him the night off and sent him to a movie," Tom replied evenly, trying to match her jovial tone. "He's been a faithful and loyal servant, you know, Miss Taylor."

Anna laughed and snuggled up close against him.

She also acted as though the unpleasantness between them that afternoon had never happened.

The old taxi seemed eager to go despite all of its mysterious grinding sounds. The steering wheel resisted Tom's efforts stubbornly but he managed to negotiate the street corners without scraping the curbs. As he wrestled the noisy taxi along the dark, rain-slickened streets, he wondered how its owner managed with just one arm and his always-present cigar. After a series of aimless turns on and off Main Street, he followed a paved street that he and Anna had taken on many previous occasions to the one and only city park. He left the main road and let the car roll down an incline onto a small graveled parking lot that overlooked Sunset Lake. It was a small, man-made lake with few trees, but it was one of the more scenic spots in the Oklahoma Panhandle and the Guymon residents were proud of it. Tom noted no other park visitors in sight as he shut off the taxicab's motor and lights.

For a moment the couple sat without saying anything, just listening in the darkness to the plink-planking of the rain on the roof of the taxi. After his eyes became more accustomed to the darkness, Tom could pick out the puckering splash marks of the rain on the surface of the lake. And inside the cab, Anna's face became excitingly visible and beautiful. He put his arm around her and pulled her over to him. She came willingly closer, her eyes serious and even darker than the night surrounding them; her dark brown hair framing the delicate face alluringly. It had been a long time since they were alone like this, and his lips found hers in a long and satiating kiss.

Finally, he leaned back against the seat and said, "We're not getting any younger."

"Speak for yourself, Doctor Bristow."

"No, I'm serious, you minx. It's not fair to either of us to be separated so long—to have to wait all these years."

She lay against his arm looking up at him wonderingly as a child would do listening to an old man tell a bedtime story. "First, you were going to marry me when we were seniors in high school, then when I finished college, then my hitch in the Army stopped that..."

"Then we were going to get married when you were discharged," Anna said, smiling half mockingly.

"And my Dad stopped that," Tom finished up for her, laughing dryly. He knew he had sounded bitter but he couldn't help it. He could still hear Benjamin Bristow's voice, "You can't study medicine with a wife and six kids hanging on your shirt-tail."

"Then mother got sick," Anna said softly, a serious, apologetic look creeping into her eyes.

He kissed her again, longer this time. She pressed hard against him and her breathing came in short gasps. Her soft, fuzzy brown sweater felt like the sleek hair of a purring kitten beneath his hand, and his fingers found intuitively the opening at the small of her back. He felt his way along the warm smoothness of her back and around to the front, reaching for her breasts. He already knew what they would be like in his mind—full and firm; he had dreamed of them many times. She squirmed, as though to pull away and then, for a tantalizing moment, relaxed against the seat as though in complete resignation. Then she pulled his hand away and said in low, patient tone, "Not yet, Tom. Not yet, my darling." Her face was a combination of protectiveness, wonderment and expectation, as though everything the world had to offer was within her reach, but that she was intentionally waiting for the right moment to grasp it.

"Sure—sure, wait—wait. We'll wake up one of these mornings and be too old to care." He sat up and started the car's motor, hating the impatience in his voice.

"Don't be angry, Tom. Wait a moment," she said, reaching over and twisting off the ignition key. "Don't walk out on me twice in one day." Her voice was calm, demanding his attention. "I'm the girl you're going to marry—remember?" She grasped his face between her hands and stuck her lips out in a teasing pout. Then, quickly, she gave him a sympathetic peck like a mother kissing a small boy.

"When?" he forced the words out.

"Just not now."

He let go of her and slid back under the steering wheel. It wouldn't do to force the issue further; that would only alienate her. No, he would play her way. He would have to let her shape him to her mold.

He started the taxi and drove her home. At her front door after he had kissed her goodbye with an explanation that he only had twenty minutes to return the taxi and catch his train, she said, "Don't give up on me, Tom. We're doing what's right. We're both doing what we have to do. Someday I can explain it better…"

Her eyes were full of a serious longing as she spoke. She didn't seem to understand after all these years that he was so much in love with her that she could cut his heart out and use it for a door mat and he would still keep coming back. He was her slave, and her will was his will. He would be patient with Anna's mother as Anna was patient, and he would be merciful to Anna's mother as Anna was merciful.

"Oh God," he thought, "will Anna ever truly be mine? Will the two of us ever be free from all the constraints, free to love each other, to marry?"

At that precise moment, he knew what he had to do, like it or not. He was going to return to the study of medicine, exactly as his father wanted. He would take the train back to St. Louis—to medical school, to the endless lectures, to the cadavers, to the smell of sickness and evil antidotes that prolonged death, to the children dying in his arms. He would ride the railed ruts that Benjamin, his proud and loving father, had charted for him long ago.

One question kept rolling over and over in his mind—"Will I ever, ever have Anna?"

Tom drove silently toward the St. Louis airport. His glistening maroon Ford Custom convertible shimmered in the evening sun. The owner of the largest car dealership in St. Louis had driven the sleek automobile to his apartment, located near the medical school, only two days ago. There was a big red ribbon tied to the steering wheel with a card attached:

To a great soon-to-be M.D. from your Father who didn't quite make it, but am proud that you did!

"You're a rare one to have somebody just give you a car like this," the car dealer had said after examining Tom's driver's license carefully, almost skeptically.

"Yeah, I'm lucky," Tom mumbled, staring at the car in disbelief. He had seen several of the new style Fords with the distinctive "spinner-type" grille and stylish body. It was another thing to actually touch and smell the luxurious interior and to hear the throaty hum of the flathead V-8 engine.

"He wired us the money—the full amount—and told us the exact model, the color and everything," the dealer said, standing with folded arms, staring first at the car and then at Tom, as though he still couldn't believe it. "We never had heard of Benjamin Bristow before. He just wired the money for the full amount. He told us the information about insurance and all, and had us write up the title and tags in your name."

The man, dressed in a tailored olive suit handed Tom the keys, ceremoniously, saying, "Well, there you go. It's just like if ole Harry Truman called us and ordered this, hisself. There's nothing else you have to do. Your ole man took care of it all. There's no payments or anything. It's all yours."

Tom remembered slipping the key into the ignition switch and twisting it, listening to the immediate response of the humming motor.

For the past two days since the dealer delivered the car, he had spent most of the time tooling around St. Louis—away from his apartment, away from the University of Saint Louis Medical School. Outwardly, he didn't appear to have a care in the world. Inwardly, he was tormented by turmoil and the impending confrontation.

Now, as the engine purred effortlessly, pointed in the direction of the St. Louis airport, he glanced around at the rich lines of the instrument panel, the luxurious carpet, all so thrillingly grand. It was more than he could have dreamed of in a thousand dreams. He had driven one of his dad's older cars occasionally while he was in high school, but only a few other students at Oklahoma University could afford a nice auto, and he didn't want to be different from the rest. Especially during his stint in the army, then during the three years of medical school, there was scant need nor time for a car.

As he drove around, drawing admiring glances, he thought to himself, "Maybe this was what Dad always meant about having money and respect."

Many times his father had said, "The only happy people in this world are those that are respected, and the only ones that are respected are the ones that have money or honor."

Tom remembered his exact words. He heard that phrase many times as he grew up, especially when Tom came back from Okinawa after WW II and his father was trying to get him to study medicine. He had hammered out the words "money and respect" so many times that Tom could remember them verbatim as they came floating up out of his subconscious now, resurrected by the new car—like prophecy in reverse.

As early as he could recall, he knew that Benjamin Bristow wasn't a person with whom you argued about such things. As a successful rancher and farmer whose vast Oklahoma Panhandle acreage included over two dozen gas and oil wells, Benjamin Bristow had much more money, honor and respect than anyone Tom had ever known.

Missouri and its sunset-bathed greenery slipped westward beneath Benjamin Bristow's small plane, a blue and white Cessna 170. Tributaries of the Mississippi river aimed their claw-like arteries eastward and, like the plane, were apparently bent on some great mission.

Benjamin peered straight ahead past the whirring McCauley fixed-pitch dual-blade, as though he expected St. Louis to pop into view at any moment. His dark eyes sparkled, intent and expectant, as he leaned forward over the controls, straining at them as if he could make the plane go faster with the force of his own weight. His jutting countenance, rigid from fifty-five years of wind and sun on the Hawk Ranch, was not conducive to conversation but his longtime friend, Amarillo's Judge Jacob Anson, was not easily deterred when it came to talking.

Flying had always made the judge a little nervous, but he never had admitted it to Benjamin. It wasn't Benjamin's handling of the plane that bothered him, for the old rancher had always been as skillful at piloting as he was at managing the Hawk Ranch, playing golf, bridge, chess or what he did best—turning a small amount of cash or resources into mountains of money.

"It's probably my big carcass being carried along so far above the ground that makes me skittish," the judge thought, and it seemed proper to him that he should talk all he pleased if it helped allay his nervousness to any degree at all.

"You'll be proud of that boy Tom when he strolls across the rostrum tomorrow at St. Louis University to get his medical degree," the judge said, smiling. "It's not everyday a man's son gets that kind of a sheepskin tacked up on his wall."

He paused, noting that Benjamin's leathery lips curled into a proud smile. He knew what the old rancher was thinking, for he had heard him say more than once that nothing else mattered to him except Tom's medical degree. How many times had he told the judge how he had failed to become a doctor himself after two years of studying medicine before his father had run off with some fine Christian woman from Hugoton, and it was left up to Benjamin to take care of his mother, brothers and sisters.

"It's not gonna happen to my son," the rancher had said again and again, each time with greater resolve. "Nothing's gonna stand in his way of getting a medical degree. Nothing or nobody!"

And now it was happening—just like Benjamin had said it would.

"I'm going to throw a celebration party for Tom tonight," the judge continued. "After all those years of studying, he's entitled to a little fun." He looked at Benjamin and waited for some response but outside of the proud twist of his lips he had to settle for a simple "yep."

"I know a night club out on Kings Highway named the Golden Goose—the Golden Slipper—or the Golden something-or-other—and it's got everything from pretty girls on down."

The judge rested his voice for a moment from the strain of talking above the plane's motor. He wanted to do something special for Tom and Benjamin. Tom's graduation was a big thing for both of them; besides, he hadn't been out with his long-time buddy Benjamin in several months and it was past time for them to pull another extravaganza. This fling with Tom would be even better than their usual trip to the Gulf Coast for fishing or a weekend of golf and chess either at Benjamin's Hawk Ranch or at the judge's home in Amarillo. For the judge, the only black spot in the picture was that his daughter Jeanie wouldn't be with them. He had tried to work it out as he had tried so many times before, but Jeanie had planned a weekend in Galveston, probably with some pimple-faced service station grease monkey. Her taste in boys had always shocked and saddened him. He had given her the best of advice since her mother died, feeling that he had to make up for the advice her mother would have given her if she had lived, as well as Jeanie's excessive preoccupation with the opposite sex. His guidance seemed doubly essential.

It was easy for him to understand why the boys would flock after Jeanie. She was beautiful, and she knew it. So different from her mother, he mused. Tom would be a good steadying influence on her—if he only knew she existed. He was too damned concerned with his studies and "that preacher's girl," as Benjamin would say.

"Benjamin, that boy of yours will make a great doctor. He's got the right temperament and the right brains for it. Another thing, he's had guts enough to stick it out long enough to get his degree, even after the years in the Army."

Benjamin kept looking straight ahead. "Yep, Judge, it looks like he's doing alright. I used to wonder about him; he was always lounging around daydreaming—especially when he came back from the Pacific after the war. You remember, he didn't want to do anything. He didn't give a damn about going to med school. He just wanted to fool around with that preacher's girl and the rest of the time he'd do nothing."

The rancher gestured emphatically with an index finger, continuing his speech full-bore: "I finally had to get tough with him, you remember, and then he decided I was right, and he settled down to his studies. These young fellows now-a-days aren't like we used to be, Judge. By God, when I was his age I had a bank account with money in it I'd earned myself. Now-a-days they don't move until you give them a shove. But one thing about Tom, when I got him started in the right direction, he kept going, and now he's going to make it."

Benjamin's voice carried well above the plane's motor. He was justified in his pride, the judge thought. Tom was a fine boy. He would do well in Amarillo if the judge could talk him into practicing medicine there.

"Jeanie tells me she hasn't been hearing much from Tom lately," the judge said. "You don't suppose he's forgotten about her altogether, do you?"

"No, he hasn't forgotten Jeanie. But you know he's always been so close to that Taylor girl, and I'm afraid they've gotten too serious about each other. I've never really known her, only met her once. She's pretty enough, but so tied down with her family. She's just not right for Tom, but he still goes to see her every time he comes home. I'm afraid it's gone too far. She's got her meat-hooks in him, and you know I've never put much stock in religion, not since my own damn Daddy took off with that nice Christian lady and never came back.

The judge looked at his lean companion and smiled. He was back on his religion kick again. Other than the occasional reference to "that nice Christian lady" who ran off with his father, Benjamin never discussed anything deeper about his bitterness against church folk. He mostly seemed to think they were all hypocrites and used their religion as a crutch to get things.

The judge didn't have a problem with religious people. He gave generously to the big downtown church and a number of Amarillo charities. He made it a point to be in the pew at least on Easter and Christmas. Other than that, he never worried about such things that might interfere with his fun and building his career. To him, it was the best of both worlds. What could be better? That's why he couldn't totally understand Benjamin's bitterness about all those who were religious.

"Well, Tom's over the age when most men get married and I think it's time he was marrying somebody." He paused, changing the subject, punching Benjamin lightly with his elbow and giving him a sly wink. "I think you know who I mean."

"Yes, I know who you mean," Benjamin said, tugging at the wide brim of his hat. "You know how much I think of Jeanie." He stopped short, reflecting.

The judge thought for a moment, then brightened: "Jeanie and I will have to come out and spend a few days with Tom and you at the ranch this summer. Maybe they'll both come to their senses."

Ben's leathery face crinkled into a half-grin for a moment and then straightened back into its usual serious lines. "By God, you're right. It's time he was deciding on a woman if he's ever going to. I was slow enough, but when I was his age I knew how to pick a woman that would help me make a go of it."

The judge laughed loudly but quit abruptly when he saw that Benjamin was serious. He was probably thinking about Erma. The farmer had picked a good one alright when he picked Erma. As a school board member, he had been part of hiring the pretty teacher from nearby Elkhart, Kansas. He watched her carefully, though distantly, as she taught the two dozen pupils at Pleasant Valley School, a one-room structure he had donated and built on the northernmost corner of the land he farmed.

He liked her strictness in handling the school children. After a year, he persuaded her to marry him. He swore it was the best thing that had ever happened to him.

The determined, hard-working blonde had helped him build the Hawk Ranch during its hungry beginnings and had stayed by him through the thirties when dust storms drove most of the Oklahoma and Texas Panhandle people off of their lands. Tom was her final contribution to Benjamin. She gave birth to their son one day without the aid of a doctor while Benjamin was in Guymon settling a land deal. Then, a few short years later, the land she had helped Benjamin acquire, turned on her and the dreaded dust pneumonia took her and made her a part of the land as it had to so many others during the Dust Bowl years. The judge had known Benjamin and Erma only casually then, but Benjamin had told him about her often.

In turn, Judge Anson had told Benjamin on occasions, rare occasions, of his own wife, Syble, mostly about the times they spent together when they were first married—the happy times. But once Benjamin had coerced him into telling him about Syble's death, a drowning accident two years before Jeanie finished high school. After Jeanie was born, Syble had become increasingly withdrawn, staying in the house day after day all to herself and utterly failing at being the wife of a public figure—the well-known attorney and county judge. Toward the end, she became so completely self-absorbed and inwardly destructive that the judge had often suspected deep within himself that her drowning was something she plotted and carried out. Of course, he had worked things out with the coroner and there was no public mention of suicide or even the possibility that she took her own life. More importantly, Jeanie had never known of his suspicions. He was glad his daughter had taken after him and learned how to enjoy life.

The first dim outlines of St. Louis appeared. Benjamin became engrossed in his landing preparations. Semi-darkness had come on them suddenly as though the little plane's juxta-movement to that of the sun had doubly quickened the latter's setting. The landing lights were turned on and the rancher and his friend glided down and landed amongst the jungle of city sounds and neon and people.

The beams of more than a dozen aircraft blinked and danced around the St. Louis Airport landing strips. Tom was only half aware of them as he wheeled his convertible into the airport parking lot. He cut off the motor and sat for a moment, once again inhaling the new-car smell and running his hand over the glossy upholstery.

Inwardly, he knew it was like caressing and lying in bed with another man's wife. The automobile's title was in his name, but it would never really be his, not even if his father said he could keep it. He rolled up the top and windows, then locked the doors, blinking at the brightness of the airport lights which were reflected in the glossy maroon finish and the tastefully placed chrome.

Inside the terminal, Tom wandered about, searching the faces of the hurrying people, half hoping he wouldn't find his father. Secretly, he wanted to get lost in the anonymous throng. At the same time, he wondered why neither he nor his father had thought to designate a more specific meeting place while they were talking to each other on the phone a week before.

Tom was about to give up finding Benjamin when he felt himself suddenly shoved unnecessarily hard from the rear. He turned around ready to give someone a verbal blast, but his anger vanished immediately when he saw that Judge Anson had done the shoving. The old man's balloon-like abdomen shook with laughter. Benjamin, looking more like a banker than a rancher, stood beside the judge, his lips curved in an amused smile.

"Judge Anson…Dad. I've been looking everywhere for you."

They shook hands.

"So Judge Anson got to come after all," he said to his father, then turned directly to the judge: "I'm glad you could make it." Tom meant it, too, because he knew the judge's levity would help get him through the evening and the next day.

"All the Rangers in Texas couldn't have kept me away from your graduation," the judge said, his heavy jowls beaming. "I just wish Jeanie could have come, too, but she couldn't get away. Believe me, she tried."

"Well, Doctor Bristow," Benjamin broke in, laying his hand on Tom's shoulder and giving the judge a proud nod of his head, "is this any way to treat your guests? I'm hungry as a coyote and thirsty as a grizzly bear, and I know the judge is, too. He always is. Why don't you lead us to that new car of yours and take us to the thickest and juiciest steaks in town."

Tom was afraid they had noticed him wince when his father called him Doctor Bristow. They apparently had not, as they went on kidding each other about who had the biggest appetite. He led them quickly out to the new car his father had given him.

Tom drove toward the Golden Slipper quietly as his father and Judge Anson discussed the car's merits in an animated fashion. Benjamin sat beside him in the front seat, and the judge sat in the rear seat, his forearms overlapping the backs of the two front seats, leaning forward so as not to miss any of the conversation, even as he made the most of it himself. When nothing else could be said about Tom's car, the judge talked of his own experiences in St. Louis—the time he watched the Cardinals "with ole Dizzy Dean and Dazzy Vance and Ripper Collins and all the Gas House Gang" play the Dodgers in 1934, his ride on the Admiral Showboat with Jeanie two years ago, and the twenty-year-old blonde bombshell dancer who seduced him at a barristers' convention in 1946. All of his stories were sprinkled impressively with dates and historical interjections about the Civil War, Louis and Clark, and even Charles Lindberg and his immortal *Spirit of St. Louis*. The judge was a hoot, there was no denying!

The Golden Slipper was crowded, but the judge was able to get a table with a good view of the floorshow which came to them in intermittent bursts of song and dance, consisting mainly of a trio of well-endowed young ladies. These women were replaced once by a couple of skaters who swirled about the postage-size ice arena, glaciered out from beneath the stage. The pair skated with reckless abandon, throwing small slivers of ice out into the audience occasionally. They were such eye-catchers they even held the judge's talk in abeyance for a time

Tom dawdled over a glass of sherry as they waited for their steaks. He was trying to keep his mind on the judge's constant chatter, and at the same time trying to think of the best way to break the news to his father.

He had tried to talk with him when it happened, then during their most recent discussion a week before. His father called him to say that he was coming to St. Louis for business, then for the graduation. It was impossible to speak with the lump lodged in his throat, so he decided it would be better to talk in person. With Judge Anson along for the ride, everything had suddenly become a bit more complicated.

Tom finally decided he was doing a poor job of both listening and thinking, so he contented himself with focusing on the girl dancers.

"Where in the hell are those steaks? They must have gone clear to Texas for them," the judge said, looking back toward the kitchen door that had swallowed up their waitress over thirty minutes ago.

"Don't complain, Judge. It was your idea to come here," Benjamin said. He winked at Tom as he spoke and tossed down the remainder of his bourbon and water.

"I was just thinking of your skinny little stomach and all of those acids eating away inside you," the judge said, chuckling.

The steaks finally came, and though the judge did most of the talking during the course of the meal, he was the first to finish eating. The Texas barrister immediately called for a bottle of port. After filling their glasses, without asking whether anyone else wanted any, he held his up to the light for a moment studying the color and fondling the glass between his plump fingers.

"The girl in the middle has a luscious mouth exactly like a woman I once represented who was suing a man for breach of contract because he reneged on his promise to marry her." Judge Anson paused, then rolled some of the wine around on his tongue for a moment. "My client was a better looking woman than she is, though," he said, studying the girl through squinted eyes as though trying to be completely equitable. "We ended the thing up by settling out of court. I finally succeeded in convincing the respondent's attorney of the woman's potential marital charms." He rolled his head round on his thick neck and smiled at Tom and his father. "She had marital charms, all right—they wound up with eight kids and are still happily married to this day!"

The judge shook the table with the raucous, uninhibited guffaws, and after another sizeable sip of wine he went on talking. He was obviously enjoying himself and seemed oblivious to the fact that Tom and his father were unresponsive, except for a polite chuckle now and then.

With the suddenness of lightening, as though to bring the judge, the floor show and everything about him to a standstill, Benjamin snapped his last bit of steak into his mouth and said, before he had finished swallowing, "Son, this graduation exercise you're having tomorrow—you'll have to tell us when and where it'll be."

Tom looked at him noncommittally, fully aware that Benjamin's thoughts were closing in on him like a knotted noose being lowered at a public hanging. The Golden Slipper had no freshly-built gallows, but the din of impending doom was as severe and certain as if it were a public square out in the Panhandle and Tom was a guilty horse thief with a black hood already draped over his head, seconds away from a swift execution.

"What are your plans after graduation?" Benjamin went on. "You haven't told me anything."

Tom didn't answer immediately. He tried to remember the things he had planned to say when the time came. That time had arrived. For a dizzying moment his mind was completely blank. He gaped at his half-eaten steak as though the answer might be found there. He felt perspiration on his forehead and he knew he had crossed the Rubicon and that there was no way of avoiding his father's questioning black eyes.

When he finally spoke, the words came gushing out like an infection that had been contained too long inside him. They were not the strong cool words of reasoning he had planned. "Please try to understand me, Dad. I know this will disappoint you—and you, too, Judge Anson, and everyone else that has ever known me—but this is the way it has to be—I won't be with the rest of my graduating class tomorrow." His voice trembled and stopped altogether for a moment before going on. "I withdrew from school a month ago—right after I wrote you the letter telling you when to come down for the graduation exercises…"

Tom paused and looked at his father, waiting for the storm to rush in upon him.

He had known the same terrifying stillness and imminent danger as a boy when he waited for the Dust Bowl storms to strike. He would stand in the front yard with his mother, watching the boiling brown clouds approach. The silence was awesome and the stillness was awesome too. The writhing dust would hunch like a serpent, slithering closer, slow, slow, slow; hovering, then devouring, grinding, tearing, smashing and smothering all life that dared to stand in the way. Then the stillness would turn yellow and dim and the shuffling clouds would be on them, straining at the limbs of the black locust trees and whipping out the juices and the green of the leaves. His mother's hand would tighten on his.

"Time we were getting in, Tommy," his mother would say, trying not to show her fear."

"No, it's not here yet," Tommy would say, dancing up and down in anticipation.

"It'll be here 'fore we can get in the house, son."

"Just a minute, Momma. You know they come slow. See the bird—it's flying away from the storm. Will it get away, Momma?"

Then the dust would be all around them, frantic and suffocating, stinging their arms and legs before they could reach the protecting walls of the house. In a little while, Benjamin would come stomping into the house, cursing the storm and yelling for a damp cloth to protect his nostrils from the choking dust. Tommy's mother would light a coal-oil lamp and his father would yell at her for taking so long, and the louder the wind howled around the clapboards that were once a bright white, the louder his father would curse the storm. His mother would listen, first to the storm outside and then to Benjamin. She would hold Tommy's head against her big soft bosom as she rocked him, holding her hands over his ears so he couldn't hear. She would watch the sand puff up through the cracks around the windows forming little drifts on the sills and covering the once fine special-made carpets and polished mahogany tables that they had ordered from Kansas City. Tom would feel her shaking and hear her quiet sobs, yet the sobs, to him, were louder than the storm. Worse, the unspoken, danger-tinged, stormy darkness in his father's eyes always seemed more terrifying than the raging storm outside.

As the horrifying duster subsided, his father would often commence to fussing around with a broom and dust pan trying to sweep up the piles of dust. Later, after the storm had died down, he would try to cheer them up. He'd talk about next fall and how they would plant again and how the rains were bound to come and settle the dust and then they could buy new carpets and repaint the house or maybe even build a new one, a brick one this time. It would have at least seven rooms, there'd be velvet carpeting and new mahogany furniture, bedrooms and all, and outside there'd be a steel-fenced yard with grass trimmed neatly like the lawns they had seen in Kansas City—green as new wheat.

Then, as if it weren't enough that the Dust Bowl continued waging its overwhelming, vicious battle for the soul of the Heartland, the dust pneumonia came to their home, hovering like an avenging, silent, shadowy-shrouded demon. Tommy was only six years old when he watched a gravedigger throw dust over his mother's coffin—dust as dry and powdery as the flour she kept in the bin that he could balance on his forearms and swing back and forth as he watched her cut out biscuits. It was dust as parched as the bank of topsoil that had covered Benjamin's young apple orchard, leaving just a few dead limbs stuck out through the hot sand. The dust was so light and chalky that Tommy wondered how they would get the mound over the grave to stay in place.

Benjamin had stood with him then with his arm around his shoulders as they listened together to the soft thudding of the dust being shoveled down on the hard boards of the coffin. Benjamin seemed to understand the deepest, most unanswerable mysteries of life back then as they stood beside the grave.

Maybe he would understand now.

Time stood still inside the Golden Slipper. The dancers were onstage again, but no one was watching them at Tom's table. The judge and his father were both staring at him as though he had lost his mind. He pushed his plate away and took a long sip of the judge's wine. The coolness of it felt good to his lips. He was successful in avoiding Benjamin's furious eyes, but he kept hoping Judge Anson would come to his rescue with some humorous remark that would clear the air of the tension that hung over them like a pall. For the first time all evening, though, the judge seemed to be without words.

Finally, Benjamin leaned forward and whispered in hoarse disbelief, "What in God's name did you say, boy? What are you trying to tell us?"

"I've decided to give up medicine," Tom said. "I don't want to get tied down to passing out pill prescriptions in one little corner of the world—there are too many other matters in the world that are more important. And my heart's just not in it anymore."

The judge was listening with his heavy jowls ajar. Benjamin sat with a stony face and fierce eyes, as though the meaning of what Tom said was at once incongruous and mind-numbing.

Tom was pleased that there was no immediate rebuttal and he pursued his argument further. "Medicine is important but it's like every other science; it is made up of guesses—just educated guesses that after many years acquire enough respect and credence that scientists start calling them facts. Then, later, when these so-called facts are proved obsolete and untrue, they are laughed at. In other words, what we know, we don't really know."

Benjamin slid his glass over to the judge for a refill of the musky port wine, staring at his son as if he were someone he had never known, a total stranger with ideas completely foreign to his own, a young man somewhat resembling himself, yet as alien as if he had suddenly dropped in from another planet.

"By god," he said in cold terse terms, "I know what I know, boy. Maybe you have no damned idea what life is like, but I do. I damn well do!"

Mockingly, the rancher turned to the judge: "How 'bout you? Do you know what you know?"

Judge Anson's stocky countenance was serious but it was obvious he appreciated the opportunity to express his views. He poured himself a fresh glass of wine. He poured with great dignity, slowly and with contemplation. Tom watched the red liquid gurgle into the glass. He needed to be concentrating on strengthening his explanation of his reasons for quitting his medical studies, but all that came to his mind was the gurgling wine, the gargled voices at the adjoining tables, the be-bop of the struggling five-piece orchestra.

Tom knew he had failed to convince Benjamin that his reasons for quitting had any reasonable merit. He also knew that he looked like an insufferable, insolent, spoiled nit-wit in the eyes of both men. He wished he could tell them about some of the things that had happened recently in emergency and operating rooms, especially the time right before Christmas when a five-year-old child, a hit-and-run victim of a drunk driver, died in his arms, and there wasn't a damned thing he could do about it.

He wished fervently that he could tell his Dad about Higa, but at the same time, he knew telling either of the other men about what happened to him in Okinawa would mean nothing to them.

Benjamin sat frozen to his chair. His shoulders sagged and his face suddenly looked older than Tom could ever remember, as if all his most prized possessions had suddenly been swept out of his reach. At the same time, there was a cold-steel defiance gleaming from his eyes and his taut lips fought back.

"You may have all these questions," the rancher said, "and your heart may not be all that enthralled with it right now, but you've wasted the last three years of your life, as far as I'm concerned. You've wasted thousands of my dollars. And what do either of us have to show for it?" The words sounded as though they had been hissed through the fangs of a snake.

"Now Benjamin," Judge Anson broke in, "let's not get upset. We're...."

"Just hold on a minute, Judge. Let the boy explain hisself," Benjamin said, glaring. "He's still got some explaining to do."

The girl singers were swaying onstage. Their melodious voices blended beautifully. The orchestra drifting back and forth from a staccato beat to a slow mumbo-bumbo sound. Jumbled voices and ice cubes clinkling on glass and the shuffling sounds of weary waiters all mixed merrily together, floating through the air like a carousel of laughing children.

"Well, it's hard for me to explain," Tom said. "You know, I'm not like you, Dad. I wish I were. I think it would be easier if I knew exactly what I was supposed to do with my life like you always seem to do."

Tom paused and looked away from his father's eyes. He hoped he was making sense, but from the disbelieving looks on Benjamin's and the judge's faces, it didn't seem likely.

"I simply don't want anything to do with medicine anymore," Tom valiantly tried to bare his deepest feelings. "I've been doing this for you, Dad. I've been doing it to honor Mother's memory. I've been doing it because I didn't know what else to do. All I know is that I couldn't do it anymore. I...I just couldn't bear to tell you. Not when I was trying to decide what to do. Not a month ago when we talked. Not even during the past week when I should have warned you what was happening to me. I couldn't tell you because I don't know the answers myself. I just have to find something more to live for...something..."

Benjamin and the judge had finished another glass of port each by the time Tom finished talking. Benjamin set his glass down and with a grin approaching sarcasm, said, "Well, I'll be go-to-hell, Judge. That was a pretty speech, wasn't it? I guess I've raised myself up a deep thinker or something."

"No, Ben, listen to the boy. Maybe you and I are just

too drunk to understand it, that's all."

Tom couldn't tell if the last remark was the truth, a snide shot, or both.

Benjamin turned down the judge's offer of another drink: "You're drunk but I'm not, and I'll be damned if I can understand a word my son is saying except that he's quitting the most important thing of his life." Turning to Tom he said with excessive curtness, "Were you failing in your grades? Wait, that couldn't be it. You've always made good grades. I can't understand it."

"My grades were good," Tom said, trying to match his father's fierce gaze. He wished he could have used poor grades as his reason for quitting school. It would have hurt Benjamin's pride, but at least he would have understood. Stupidity was one thing, yet lack of direction was simply unforgivable for a Bristow.

"So, what are you going to do with yourself, boy?" Benjamin spat out the words. Benjamin's voice dripped with bitterness and disappointment, and it was apparent how he was already thinking how he would have to face his friends back in the Panhandle, all the people to whom he had shared the dream he had for his son.

Tom fidgeted with his napkin. He wasn't sure himself what he would do with his new-found freedom. He might as well forget about Anna as long as her mother was alive, especially since poor Anna hadn't found her freedom yet—she didn't know what it was like to do what she wanted to do. Higa had found hers and she had something else besides freedom, something immeasurable like no one else he had ever met.

Higa!

He knew he would go see her. She was so far away. It would take money, more money than he had. Whatever it took, he would find a way to go see Higa and find out once and for all what she was talking about.

"I'd be glad to come out and work at the Hawk Ranch for awhile as I figure out what's next for me." Tom was surprised at his own words.

"I don't want your help," Benjamin said tartly. "I'm afraid it might turn out like your medical degree...or lack of it. Once a quitter, always..."

Instantly Benjamin regretted his final words, but he was not the sort of man to take anything back. Still, his tone softened: "You're welcome to stay at the Hawk Ranch as long as you want, just as long as you stay away from that preacher's girl in Guymon. That girl is no good. I've got a sneaking suspicion she's just waiting around for me to die so she can get my money. Her father never worked a day in his life and never owned anything that somebody didn't give him."

The rancher was back in control: "By God, I won't stand for you getting mixed up with that kind even though you've turned out to be a failure yourself!"

The flash had returned to Benjamin's eyes and he snapped out his words with a coldness and sharpness that cut straight to the mark.

"If I ever hear of you going out with that preacher's girl, I'll have the judge here fix it so you won't get a penny when I'm gone, not so much as a damned prairie dog hole."

Each word gouged its way into Tom's conscience with the sharpness of a scalpel. He didn't mind his father ranting about Anna and her parents anymore. He had heard it so many times he was beginning to believe it himself. He didn't mind that. And it wasn't the prospects of losing his inheritance in the Hawk Ranch that hurt. But it was the fear Tom was feeling for the first time that his new freedom was already costing him too much, more than he wanted to pay.

Suddenly, he realized that he was all alone, though all three men sat at a table in the midst of the Golden Slipper's frivolity. Just as if he were using a hacksaw, his father's words were sundering the bond that had held him and his father together all his life. He wanted to reach across the table and touch the muscular arm of his father and feel the warmth that he used to find there. But he couldn't do it. The chasm between them was widening. It was already un-crossable, as though they stood on opposite cliffs of a precipice, looking across at each other, hoping that somehow the other one would find a way to cross over.

The rift had begun forming the summer before Tom started medical school. It happened the night his father ordered him not to marry Anna. Now, at this very moment, it was as if the earth's foundations had shifted, leaving a gaping vastness between him and his father.

"You don't need to worry about Anna Taylor," Tom said, trying to keep his voice even. "She turned me down once. She won't marry me as long as her mother lives. Her mother's an invalid, you know, and Anna thinks no one else can take care of her. Mrs. Taylor's heart condition just keeps getting worse, and for nearly three years the doctor has been warning them that she doesn't have long to live. Still, she keeps hanging on. Anna's nothing but a slave to her, and I couldn't care less about any of them anymore."

Tom knew his lie was unconvincing. He knew he sounded like a spoiled brat. It didn't matter. In the end, his words had gone unheard. The judge had turned and was watching the skaters. Benjamin was staring across Tom's shoulder at nothing in particular. The moment had passed. Life had changed forever. All three men at the table knew it, yet each wanted to ignore what had just happened.

Tom knew there was no use going into more detail about what his plans were. He couldn't tell them about Higa, nor Okinawa, until he found out the truth about her himself. She had grown, especially this past month, into an ever increasing hunger within him crying to be filled. Perhaps everyone has that same desire within him that yearns for a Higa. But most men never find her. They let her drift away beneath the flotsam of unpursued dreams. Tom determined that he would not let this happen.

But Tom could tell his father nothing of this. The chasm was far too wide. Any verbalized thoughts, at this point, would fall into the depths between them.

There was disappointment mixed with anger in the old man's eyes. It must be like wormwood to him, Tom thought. And he refilled his father's glass with wine, hoping to wash away or at least dilute the bitterness on his father's tongue.

4

The next morning Tom watched the St. Louis skyline shrink out of sight in his rear-view mirror. The sun gleamed down on the hood of his new convertible as the flathead engine hummed smoothly. He had never driven the 700 miles between St. Louis and the Hawk Ranch before. There was no need for a car during the pressure-packed years of medical school. He had always traveled back and forth by plane or train. Still, it wasn't hard to see that all he had to do was point the nose of the Ford Custom down Highway 50 to Jefferson City, then head West via Highway 54 past Wichita, Pratt, Meade, Liberal, across the State Line into Oklahoma, then home.

The long trip might give him time to sort out what had just happened. His father had refused a ride to the airport. Instead, he and the judge took a taxi. It was probably better that way. The silence during the last part of the previous evening had been deafening. Chilling. A funeral with no dead bodies.

Tom snapped on the radio, waited a moment for it to warm up, then settled on a station playing popular tunes. He leaned back, stretching his arms full length against the steering wheel. It was a wonderful feeling; fleeting along with no cares, doing as he pleased; no studies—no classes to meet this morning.

The words from the Hank Snow song, belting from his radio speaker, seemed especially ironic:

But someday baby when you've had your play
You're gonna want your daddy but your
daddy will say
Keep movin' on,
you stayed away too long
I'm through with you,
too bad you're blue
Keep movin' on.

Patti Page's lilting soprano replaced Hank Snow's gravely baritone. She sang, "Tennessee Waltz."

"Why do all the good tunes seem to be about sadness, losing and leaving?" he said out loud, his voice lost in the Missouri wind.

His mind was temporarily diverted for a few moments as a succession of comedic Burma Shave signs swept past:

On curves ahead

    Remember, sonny

        That rabbit's foot

            Didn't save the bunny

                BURMA-SHAVE

He grinned briefly, then returned to his thoughts. Benjamin had let him keep his car. His Dad had merely shrugged his shoulders, stone-faced, when Tom offered him the keys.

"You can keep it," the rancher snapped. "I keep my word whether you do or not. Besides, it's probably the only new car you'll ever drive."

Tom winced again as he felt the stabbing pain from his father's words. It was expected, though. In time, perhaps when he arrived at the Hawk Ranch, it might all blow over.

Whether it did or not, Tom only planned to stay there temporarily until he could figure out how to make enough money to fly to Okinawa. He'd taken what was still left in his St. Louis bank account. It was enough to survive for awhile, but not enough to do what he was already planning.

By mid-afternoon Tom had left behind the rolling hills and curves of Missouri, and had crossed into Kansas near Fort Scott. Highway 54 was relatively free of traffic as he whipped along the increasingly flat pastures and wheat lands. He stayed overnight at a travel lodge on the outskirts of Wichita. By nine the next morning, he was heading west again, and by early afternoon, he crossed into Oklahoma just south of Liberal.

The state line signaled the north edge of the Oklahoma Panhandle, No Man's Land, 167 miles long and about 34.5 miles wide, totaling more than 3,500,000 acres.

Lured by the promise of a fresh start on free land, Tom's Grandpa, Jedediah Bristow had left behind Kentucky's bluegrass pastures with his young family not long after the Organic Act of 1890 placed No Man's Land in the new Oklahoma Territory.

Tom's father, Benjamin, was born in a one-room dugout home two years later. When Oklahoma Territory and Indian Territory joined the Union in 1907 as the single state of Oklahoma, Beaver County was divided into Beaver, Texas and Cimarron counties. It was a place of history for Tom. Benjamin, forced to leave his own medical studies and take over his father's farm in his early twenties, had built the Hawk Ranch into one of the biggest and most admired enterprises in all of Texas County. He enjoyed breaking open the buffalo grass and turning the hidden riches beneath it into wealth. He learned to ignore the rattlesnakes, droughts, coyotes, dust storms and blizzards. Benjamin added to his land holdings by purchasing large blocks of adjoining fields at low prices from neighbors who left for a myriad of reasons.

Tom felt an instinctive closeness to the land where two generations of Bristows before him had carved out a living from the often-unforgiving sod.

He breathed deeply, filling his lungs with the arid, often-fragrant winds that swept endlessly over the Plains.

He had almost forgotten how green the wheat grows in the Panhandle during late May. As many times as he had left and returned to the Hawk Ranch, he was always amazed at the flatness of the land. Most people would consider it dull and lifeless, but to him there was always a thrill in returning to it. It was a land of uninhibited distance, wide skies, a place of incredible freedom that he had found nowhere else during his travels during his college years, then World War II, or during the three years of medical school. He knew that wherever he went, his feeling for this flat land and his sense of belonging to it would never die out altogether.

As he drove southwest, he saw the mileage marker with the name Guymon on it, bringing flittering flashbacks of the town nearest the Hawk Ranch and its origins. Sometime during the 1890s, a man named Edward T. Guymon purchased a section of land west of the Beaver River, the eventual site for the fledgling town that would bear his name. After the Chicago, Rock Island and Pacific Railway built tracks through the No

Man's Land hamlet during 1901 and started passing through regularly, the town began growing rapidly. Initially named Sanford, it was renamed after the founder as railroad officials sought to avoid any confusion with Stratford, Texas, forty one miles southwest down the rail line. Guymon incorporated in 1905, two years before Oklahoma attained statehood.

Warm memories of his childhood home helped the remaining miles to slip rapidly beneath the wheels of Tom's car. The closer he got to Guymon, the more he kept thinking of Anna.

Inwardly, he kept trying to push her out of his mind, to replace her with the rolling sea of wheat all about him, to let the bright blue of the sky with its little wisps of clouds take her place, to think about Higa. But nothing sustained his thoughts, and Anna kept coming back, pulling him toward her like a magnet.

Back in St. Louis at the Golden Slipper, after Benjamin threatened to cut him out of his inheritance if he saw Anna, he had told his father and the judge that he was through with her and that it would be easy to forget her. He meant the words as they came out of his mouth. As he neared Guymon, he knew he had lied to his father, to the judge and to himself. There was no staying away from her as long as there was any hope for a future together, no matter what his father said.

Turning a deaf ear to his own words, as well as his father's dire threat, he decided to chance a visit to Anna house.

He had never passed through Guymon without seeing her, and Benjamin wouldn't be back at the Hawk Ranch for another day. He had flown the judge to the University of Texas to see Jeanie, then to Amarillo. Austin was six hundred miles southeast of the ranch. Amarillo was more than a hundred miles south of Guymon.

"There'll be plenty of time to see her before Dad gets back," he thought out loud, "not that seeing Anna will do any good."

Anna would be nice, of course, and admirably patient, but she was locked into the same world in which she had apparently been destined to live. Yet he wanted to see her because he had to. It was that simple. As he drove down Guymon's Main Street, he turned the steering wheel toward the Taylor house.

"I'll let you drive it," Tom said, gesturing from Anna's front porch toward his shiny new convertible, "but you have to promise not to go over eighty!"

He laughed inwardly, knowing that the last thing Anna would do was drive over the speed limit under any circumstances. At the same time, he tightened his arm around her waist, wondering if his face showed the disappointment he felt at the hasty, almost casual kiss Anna had just given him. She must have found out about his quitting school. He knew she would be disappointed, almost as much as Benjamin, but he hadn't expected her to react with such coolness.

Anna looked at the beautiful maroon convertible, smiling at his attempted humor. "It's a beauty, Tom," she said, too seriously. "I wish I could go with you, but…you know I can't leave Mother here alone. Father's out making some calls. She might need me."

Her face was unusually pale, almost gaunt, as she spoke, and Tom felt like lifting her up and carrying her to his car, then pirating her away from these grim surroundings that were slowly destroying the healthy, happy Anna he used to know.

"Won't she be all right for a little while?" Tom asked, nodding toward the back part of the house where her mother lay. "A little sun and relaxation would do you good."

But even as he spoke Anna was reaching for the door

handle to go back inside the house. He followed her through the front room and down the long, drab hall that led to her mother's bedroom. As they passed her door, Anna put her finger to her lips signifying that her mother was asleep. Tom could see the willowy figure under the bed covers, and he could hear the muted breathing as they walked by softly, careful lest the worn linoleum would make a waking noise.

Anna motioned for him to follow as she entered the kitchen.

"It's time for me to start fixing her supper," she whispered. "Won't you stay and eat with us." She smiled at him briefly. Tom started to reach for her hand, but she walked rapidly past him and started taking groceries out of the cupboard.

"I have a stew on that will be done in a few minutes," she said, straining to reach a stack of bowls. Her reddish brown hair caught the late afternoon sun as it streamed through the window, and it looked for a moment as though she were wearing a golden crown.

"It's the kind you like, Tom," she added after getting the bowls from the cabinet.

It would have been so wonderful, just the two of them, eating together in this small kitchen. They could laugh and talk about nothing at all or the world's greatest mysteries, much like they used to, and then they could go out for a ride in his car, maybe see a movie. That's what they would have done ten years ago or even five years ago. But not now. Her mother was lying only a few feet away, a hopeless barrier that had come between them. He could see her through the open doorway, motionless with gnarled wrists poking grotesquely out from under the sheets. Her face was anemic and expressionless. She was sickly grey and utterly dying, undeserving of the care that Anna continued to give her.

He stopped his thoughts, knowing they were horrible, unspeakable and selfish. He also knew it was pointless to try to tell Anna that she was killing herself slaving after her mother. He had tried to talk to her about it before, but she wouldn't listen then, and she wouldn't listen now.

"No. I can't stay. I've got to be going," Tom said suddenly, without looking at Anna. He started walking back through the house toward the front door. Tears burned his eyelids, and he tried to blink the scalding droplets away. He heard Anna following him. As he passed through the front door, she pulled at his arm, a look of concern brimming over in her eyes.

"Where are you going, Tom?" She almost shouted the words.

"I'm going out to the Hawk Ranch. Then I don't know where I will go. All I know is that I'm going to start living again."

He turned his head so she wouldn't see his red eyes. He wanted to tell her about the new freedom he was going to start enjoying now that he had given up medicine and all its accompanying headaches and pressures, but he knew she wouldn't understand.

Instead, he merely repeated the phrase, "All I know is that I'm going to start living again." Then he added, "with or without you."

Instantly he wished he could take back the last four words. Anna's face dropped as though he had struck her with his fist. He wanted to take the words back, but he knew it was impossible. He had spoken the words. She had heard him, undeniably heard him.

Suddenly he wanted to get away. He wanted to be free of Anna, her sick mother, and the cold linoleum floors of the Taylor's house. He wanted to be free of her father, too, the dignified pastor. He wanted to get away from this parsonage that sat next to the place where all the self-righteous religious people met again and again. Whether Benjamin was right about Anna and her father, he didn't care. He wanted to forget them all.

Tom told Anna goodbye—without kissing her—and his new car's fast departure lifted a cloud of rubber, gas fumes and dust that drifted toward her as she stood motionless on the front porch, settling down upon her like a shroud as she watched him drive around the corner and out of sight.

There was a parking place directly in front of Lonnie's Pool Hall. Tom impulsively whipped his car into the opening. He had driven around Guymon for awhile after leaving the parsonage, then had sat beside Sunset Lake for some time, trying to sift through everything that had happened.

Finally, he decided to drop by Lonnie's. There was still plenty of time to get out to the Hawk Ranch before bed-time. The long drive from St. Louis and the ordeal at Anna's house had left him feeling achingly empty and incredibly thirsty.

The sounds of clacking pool balls and men yelling and laughing came to him from the rear of the pool hall. Tom walked in and sat down at the lunch counter. The bald-headed short-order man that Tom had seen so many times before strode over from his place by the front window. It was where he always stood when there were no customers, one foot propped on the window sill, picking at his teeth and staring out at Guymon's Main Street activities. The old man drummed his fingers impatiently on the counter as he waited for Tom's order as though anxious to fill it and get back to his sentry position by the window.

"I'd like a draw beer—a large one."

"One large draw coming up." He drew the beer expertly, holding the glass so the golden stream hit its side at the proper angle. "Anything else?" he asked, sliding the beer along the counter toward Tom.

"What's good to eat?" Tom asked hesitantly as he scanned the grease-dimmed menu on the wall behind the counter.

"Everything's good. The special today is knuckles and kraut."

"That's what I want," a loud voice to Tom's left butted in. Tom turned to see who was sitting down beside him and almost jumped when he recognized the pudgy, red-faced man as the bully who had so mercilessly beat up the skinny guy the last time he was there. Tom shuddered when he remembered the nights he had spent in restless agony trying to forget the fat, twisted lips that always seemed to be saying, "It's not forty-seven…it's forty-nine!" Then the big eyes of the skinny one would take Willie's place on the dark stage at the foot of his bed and would say in his nasal-complaining voice as though talking through a broken nose, "No, it's forty-seven, the same as mine. We tied. You can count mister—what do you say the score is?" Then his face would dance before him in a ridiculing blend of accusing hatred and whimpering pleading, screaming over and over, "What do you say the score is? Tell him—what do you say the score is? We tied. Tell him—tell him—tell him."

"I'm Willie Lusby," bellowed the pudgy-faced man who had just sat down beside Tom. "I've seen you around here from time to time, and I feel like I ought to know you. I just can't recollect your name right now." He stuck his large fleshy hand out to Tom as he spoke.

Tom shook hands with him and said with considerable curtness, "Tom Bristow."

"Any relation to Benjamin Bristow?"

"Yes, he's my father."

The waiter jostled the plates of knuckles and kraut down on the counter before Tom and his friendly neighbor, then resumed his stance by the window, once again picking his teeth, eyes darting from movement to movement on the street outside.

Willie's lips twisted into a grin. He laughed hoarsely and briefly before saying, "By God, that's a good one. I was just on my way out to his place to go to work for him. He just up and fired his top guy, and he wants me to be his harvest foreman this year."

He paused long enough to fork in a couple of oversized bites of pigs knuckles before turning his fat, greasy lips back to Tom. "You going to help in the harvest?" His eyes swept briefly over Tom, obviously doubting his capabilities to do anything involving work.

Tom took a bite of the pig's knuckle, aware that Willie was sizing up his tender white hands, comparing them to his own calloused, red ones. He was undoubtedly also comparing the silk sport shirt that Tom had bought in one of St. Louis' finest men's clothing stores with his own faded blue denim shirt.

"I might help some," Tom said, fearful that he had sounded too nervous and uncertain.

Willie went back to mauling his pig knuckles, holding the bone in his hand now and gnawing over its greasy surface with loud sucking sounds that could be heard all over the front part of the pool hall. Finally, he stopped to tear a large slice of bread apart and sop at the juice in his plate. "Last year, I run a crew for a big spread down by Dalhart. The old man that owns it told me I could get more work out of a man than Simon Legree hisself. I guess your dad must have got wind of my reputation when he needed somebody to take over?" He laughed noisily and punched Tom in the side with his elbow.

Tom drank the rest of his beer and stood up. He had lost interest in his pig's knuckles and kraut, as well as jawing any more with a man whom he disliked. "I've got to be going,' he said, walking toward the cash register.

"Say, boy, the thought just struck me. I was planning on getting a buddy to drive me over to your Dad's ranch. If you're heading out there tonight anyway, I hope you don't mind me hooking a ride with you."

Willie laughed his short hoarse laugh and walked over to the cash register with Tom as though it were all settled.

Tom did mind, but that didn't seem to matter.

"Sure, come along," Tom said, wishing he had the courage to simply tell him the truth—that he didn't want to be around Willie tonight, tomorrow or ever. Then, knowing he could never say those words, he placated himself by deciding that the noisy fellow might be of considerable value in helping him forget about Anna during the ride to the Hawk Ranch. Besides, it looked like Tom was going to have to get acquainted with the massive bully, whether he wanted to or not.

5

The familiar, ageless excitement of returning home grew in Tom's throat as he turned into the Hawk Ranch drive-way. The two large cedar posts that guarded either side of the entrance welcomed him like old friends as he passed through.

He wondered if Benjamin still felt the same way, or if he had cooled down during the past few days. Maybe some of his fatherly disappointment had melted away. Regardless, excitement pounded away within him as he drove on up the drive. He heard the announcer on his car radio say it was ten-thirty as he turned into the drive of the Hawk Ranch.

Apparently Benjamin had arrived from St. Louis, via Austin and Amarillo, right on schedule. One of the garage stalls was vacant and the door was open. Tom hesitated to drive his car into the space, so he decided to park outside the garage.

"Still," he thought, "if Benjamin did leave it open for me, it might be a good sign."

He and Willie got out of the car. The new foreman grabbed his drab-green war-surplus knapsack out of the back seat and followed Tom to the front door.

The house was dark except for the walnut paneled office where Benjamin often sat up late at night going over his financial records and where he kept his huge safe containing his abstracts, insurance policies and other valuables. He also kept large quantities of currency there, too, a leftover idiosyncrasy, to Tom's way of thinking, after losing a fortune in the aftermath of Black Tuesday's Stock Market crash on October 29, 1929. The bank closings left Benjamin wary and distrustful of any institution, governmental or otherwise. The years of the Great Depression, even after the Stock Market bottomed out during 1932, only added to Benjamin's distrust of banks, stocks and high finance.

The air was rich with the scent of black locust blossoms as Tom and Willie Lusby walked up to the front door. It was unlocked; Benjamin had never believed in locking doors. Like other Plains pioneers, he believed honesty and character made locks unnecessary.

Tom opened the door and motioned Willie to follow him in. His gesture was unnecessary, since Willie was already hard on Tom's heels, eager-eyed. Tom opened the door leading into the den from off the entrance-way rather apprehensively. He had always wondered how he would react if he came home and found a burglar in the act of ransacking the place, rather than the elder Bristow conducting business.

But he needn't have worried. His father wheeled around from his kneeling position by the safe, angry eyed. Green currency was in neat stacks on the floor in front of him. Tom felt Willie's heavy breaths on his neck and turning, saw that his eyes glowed with excitement and his lips were twisted into a greedy grin.

"Dammit boy," Benjamin yelled sharply at Tom, "haven't you learned how to knock yet?" He bent down and tossed the money hurriedly into the safe and snapped the door shut.

"I'm sorry, Dad. I thought you planned to be with the judge and didn't think you would be here until tomorrow. I thought it might be you when I saw the light on, but wanted to make sure."

Benjamin gave the combination dial a quick flip, ignoring Tom's apologies.

"I've brought Willie Lusby out with me," Tom tried to break the steely silence. "I happened to bump into him in town, and he told me you planned to use him to run your harvest crew this summer."

Benjamin got up from his knees, walked quickly over to Willie and shook hands with him.

"I wasn't expecting you until tomorrow," the rancher said, his voice softening a bit, "but it's all right. I've got the best crew in the Southwest lined up for you, and we've got a lot to do while we're waiting for the wheat to ripen. In fact, we've got some fields that are already beginning to turn."

"Yessir, Mr. Bristow. I noticed that myself on the way out, and I'll be ready to start when you say the word." Willie pumped his new employer's hand vigorously.

"I think it can wait `til morning," Benjamin said, gruffly trying to be humorous. "C'mon with me, and I'll show you where you're going to sleep."

The two of them walked off in the direction of the bunkhouse, leaving Tom alone. He walked around the room examining small items with which he had grown up—a picture of his mother that Benjamin always kept prominently on his desk, a small porcelain vase Benjamin had brought home from Kansas City shortly before Tom's mother died, though it didn't appear any flowers had been placed in it since she passed away.

The most incongruous object, though, and the one that always intrigued Tom was a large Bible that had belonged to his mother. It had her name engraved in gold on the front cover. To Tom's knowledge, Benjamin never opened it, yet he kept it nearby. Tom had looked through it many times, especially at the genealogy entries his mother had penned. Occasionally Tom had even attempted to read the Scriptures, too, as he had seen his mother do every day. Regrettably, he usually began with Genesis and stopped about the time Adam and Eve left the Garden of Eden.

There were many reminders of his mother in the room. The main objects that spoke volumes about his father were the massive desk, cavernous safe and the treasured contents inside the lock-box.

Tom sat down in his father's chair and stretched his legs out before him. It was good to be home again. He could sleep as long as he pleased in the morning. No more classes—no more cadavers. It was a free world—his own big, free world.

The next morning Tom met Harriett Elston. She was the latest in a series of Benjamin's housekeepers. Most of them seemed to tolerate Benjamin's curt and demanding ways for only a couple of months. Sometimes they only lasted a couple of days. One woman named Prudence Perkins had endured exactly twenty-three minutes of the old man's meanness before stomping out the door and heading back to wherever she came from. By a whopping five minutes, good ole Prudence beat the then-record time belonging to a lady named Gladys Seidletz, though Gladys had made a much more dramatic departure by deliberately dropping an armload of plates at Benjamin's feet before huffing out the door.

Tom noticed that Harriett had one advantage over the others: She was hard of hearing, either truthfully or selectively. She went about her duties in a dogged manner, either not hearing Benjamin's unpleasantries or ignoring them. The house was in the best order Tom could remember seeing it, and her breakfast of ham and eggs, cooked to perfection, and wild blackberry rolls delighted Tom's palate. He hadn't eaten much the day before, so he gorged himself until he finally had to stop eating out of sheer self-preservation.

Benjamin had little to say during the meal except to growl at Harriett for more coffee a couple of times. She seemed to hear him well on those occasions and brought the java to him promptly. It was only when he yelled out comments that were critical of her food or something not demanding an immediate responsive action that she ignored him.

"Why didn't you put your car in the garage last night?" Benjamin asked, staring at Tom accusingly as though he had committed some kind of a misdemeanor.

"I wasn't sure you meant for me to use it, Dad." He tried not to sound combative, but wasn't sure if he was successful. He wasn't sure himself why he hadn't used the open space.

Benjamin scooted his chair back from the table, stood, looked directly at his son, then quipped, "I wouldn't have left the damned door open if I didn't want you to use it."

He threw the last comments over his shoulder as he walked off hurriedly toward his office. He was back, attaché case in hand, before Tom had finished eating. He leaned over the stove where Harriett was standing, telling her matter-of-factly that he was going to get Willie and the crew started, then he was heading to Amarillo on business and wouldn't be home until late that night or the next day. His lips almost touched her ear as he yelled the words.

Tom went to the kitchen window and watched his father stride quickly across the yard. He spoke with Willie for a few moments, made several gestures, then stepped toward the hangar where he kept his Cessna 170. There was enough Bristow child in him that he wanted to run after his Dad and ask him if he could go with him.

"I don't think so," Tom mused to himself. The rancher would have loved to have his son ride along 'then' years ago, and maybe even a month or a week ago. Not now. The chasm continued widening. Apparently it would take a while to get over his bitterness, if ever.

"Let him go," Tom muttered. "Let him fly around in his airplane awhile, and he will soon forget how much I have disappointed him."

Tom rubbed his eyes on his forearm. A couple of men were pushing the plane out of the hanger and onto the lap of the pasture that Benjamin used for a runway. It was a long strip of buffalo grass that lay alongside a part of the golf course that Benjamin had built and kept watered religiously.

Benjamin climbed into the Cessna. The dual-blade propeller flashed in the sunlight. The plane roared down the narrow strip of asphalt, then the aircraft rose easily, effortlessly over the wheat fields and buffalo grass into the bright morning sky. It arced off to the south toward Amarillo, then blended into the heavens.

So many times he had watched his father fly away into the horizon. He often wondered what would happen if his father never returned from a flight someday, especially after his mother died. He often prayed, much as his mother had done so many times, for his father's safety as he flew. And always his father had returned unharmed.

Tom looked across his shoulder to see if Harriett was watching him. She wouldn't understand why he was red-eyed thinking about his mother and father, especially the days gone by. Or would she? Maybe she and her father had a contorted relationship, too. She was so strangely aloof, so wrapped up in herself and her work.

Harriett bent low over the kitchen sink and seemed unaware that he was still there at all, let alone noticing his misty eyes. She seemed oblivious to everything except the task that was before her. She was wrestling with a huge black skillet, scrubbing and shining at it with painstaking diligence, as though it were the only thing on earth that mattered.

"Poor ignorant woman," Tom thought. "She will live out her days knowing nothing but household slavery—doing petty jobs that anyone could do. And it's not like Dad cares a whit. Poor, foolish, lost woman."

Except for the scraping and splashing noises of Harriett's pans in the sink, the house was like a tomb. It was as if Benjamin had taken all the life and vitality of the Hawk Ranch with him. After the blue sky swallowed him up, there were no more sounds, no color, no activity, no life left until he returned.

Tom was used to the clattering and roaring noises of St. Louis traffic, students chattering, the rush of their scuffling feet in the halls between classes. After a couple of hours the quietness that permeated the Hawk Ranch began to stifle him. It was good to have no duties, no one requiring something of him, but yet he couldn't help feeling annoyed at all this vast silence.

He went outside and walked from one outbuilding to another, stopping first at the well house and then the nearby windmill. He noted with satisfaction that a pipe running parallel to the ground, about four feet above the ground, was still smooth with a darker polish to it than the rest of the pipe. That was from his own gymnastics as a boy, especially "skinning the cat."

Ah, those were the days of true freedom, even though Benjamin hadn't liked for him to play on the pipe. In fact, his father had spanked him once for dislodging the pipe from a brace that held it over the cattle watering tank.

Today, there were fewer cattle. Since the riggers had discovered gas and oil wells on his land, Benjamin had long since sold off the bulk of his herd and concentrated more on growing wheat. He kept some purebred Herefords and Angus cattle around, but they were more for old time's sake than profit.

Tom smiled as he looked at the shiny water pipe. The windmill still stood but obviously didn't run as much as before. Tom unleashed the brake handle and watched the tail swing out and direct the blades of the wheel into the mild breezes. He was relieved at the groaning sounds of the sucker-rod as it jabbed itself deep into the earth. Soon the gurgling sounds signaled water as it poured from the end of the pipe in spasmodic spurts to match the drawing action of the sucker-rod deep below. The harmony, the way the well worked, was like a majestic melody, as unique as the vast silence all around him.

He watched the water spurting out and listened to its tinkling splashes for a long time, then those sounds blended into the surroundings. It became a part of the windmill groanings, the quiet air and Harriett's pans in the sink. It all came to Tom's ears in one humming harmony that seemed to urge him to do something, to move, to be free, to live. He walked away from the well house and the windmill. Finally he could no longer hear the water running.

He passed by the other buildings quickly—the old barn that had been converted to a wheat granary; the hog sheds and chicken-house, unused for years but freshly painted and durable looking, the bunkhouse that at night resounded with the curses, card playing and raucous laughter of a varying assemblage of grizzled hired hands. The number of the crew depended upon the season of the year. It was all quiet in the bunkhouse now as the men were all out working, preparing for the harvest.

The main change since Tom had last spent any significant time on the farm was the new machine shed. It was five times as large as any of the other Hawk Ranch buildings. It was covered with silver-colored sheet metal that shone like a mirror in the sun. It wasn't until

Tom approached it that he noticed the hired hands and Willie Lusby. All except the latter were swarming over the giant harvesting machines that were commonly called "combines." The men worked knowingly, tightening a bolt here, greasing a bearing there, getting the machines ready for the harvest. Willie strode about between the machines shouting instructions to the men, hands in pockets.

Nearby stood more unconstructed mounds of shiny metal, apparently what would become additional granaries for the bumper crop Benjamin anticipated.

Tom stopped while he was still fifty yards away. He would see the new machine shed and the soon-to-be granaries some other time when Willie Lusby wasn't around. Fortunately, the new harvest crew leader hadn't seen him, so Tom turned and walked back to the house.

"There's a little coffee left on the stove," Harriett said to him as he entered the kitchen. She was shaping the crust of a pie and didn't look up as she spoke.

"Oh, thanks, but I have some unpacking to do right now—maybe later."

Actually, it was the packing, not unpacking, on which he wanted to concentrate. He would be leaving for Okinawa as soon as he could sort everything out. But in the meantime, he needed to put away all the things he had brought back with him from nearly three years in St. Louis.

Unpacking his suitcases was a slow and tedious task, and soon it became obvious to him he would be short of closet space. He began throwing aside all items he didn't think he would need.

Then he saw some old boxes hovering at the back side of a high shelf almost obliterated in dust and darkness. He pulled them down and untied the twine that had held their straining sides together so many years. He went through them hurriedly, lifting out piece by piece all the shirts, trousers, underclothes, shoes, mittens and all types of clothing he had worn as a boy. The smaller sizes, those he wore before his mother died, were mostly threadbare and of inexpensive cloth, the ones he wore before the oil and gas wells were discovered. The larger sizes were the best that Benjamin's money could buy. Tom passed over those quickly, remembering how the pretentious buttons and stitches had made him feel out of place with the other children.

At the bottom of one box, his hand felt something rough and hard, and pulling it out from beneath the clothes, he remembered it immediately as the toy doctor's kit his father had bought him when he was ten years old. He smiled as he recalled how he had taken out all of the kit's contents and used the bag for a fishing tackle case.

Knocking at his door interrupted his thoughts. Tom opened it and Harriett came in carrying a tray of food. Besides the pie she brought lemonade, hot rolls, acorn squash and pork chops.

He glanced at his wristwatch and was amazed to see that it was noon.

"You didn't have to bring it to me, Harriett," Tom said as he pulled a small table over to a chair and cleared the top of it so she would have a place to set the tray. "But I'm famished and glad to see the food." He took a bite and then, as an after-thought, said, "Why don't you join me."

Harriett shook her head no and smiled. It was the first time Tom had seen her smile. It seemed to change her whole personality; several gold crowns showed through and added to the warmth of her smile.

"I've got a lot of cleaning to do in Mr. Bristow's room and I want to get it done while he's gone," she said, turning to leave.

"Don't leave...I'm in need of a little help...I can't figure out what to do with all these old clothes." He waved an arm in the direction of the scattered stacks of apparel.

Harriett sat down. She said nothing, a look of uneasiness on her face.

"Mmmm," Tom murmured dramatically, "these pork chops are delicious."

Harriett still didn't speak. She just sat on the edge of her chair, hands folded in her lap, her warm smile flooding her face. Tom looked at her angular frame and wondered about her family, if she had ever borne a child or known a man. The idea seemed preposterous to him somehow that this square-shouldered, flat-chested woman could have ever slept with a man. She must have a million secrets locked within her sallow skin from her fifty years or more of living. It was such a waste—all her thoughts and all the things she had ever done. Everything would eventually come to nothing like all the thoughts and doings of his mother, Benjamin, even Anna and Willie and all the rest. They would all end up like his mother, dust in the ground for future generations to trod upon.

"It's sad that these should all go to waste," Harriett said suddenly as she bent over to straighten a shirt in the box nearest her.

"You mean the clothes," Tom's mind raced. He realized she was talking about the clothing. "Yes, it's sad," Tom said, draining the last of his lemonade and getting up from his chair. "I'd better get them boxed up. Maybe you can give them to some charity or church or..."

Anna's church? Even talking about old clothing made him think of her. He forced himself to listen to Harriett's words.

"Yes," she said, "and I'd better get started on Mr. Bristow's room or I mayn't have a job when he comes back." She picked up the food tray.

Tom laughed. "I don't think you have to worry about that." He thought of the others who hadn't lasted nearly as long. She seemed to have figured out the secret to working with his father.

She smiled briefly and left with the tray. Later, he heard her moving about his father's room, buzzing with the electric sweeper near the walls separating them. He resumed sorting and repacking and hanging his clothes.

In a back corner, he spied the Army dress uniform that hung in the closet—brass buttons still shining, with medals and corporal stripes in place—all just like he hung it the first day he returned from Okinawa and his honorable discharge on the West Coast. He felt the material and fingered the medals that had been won with such deep pride. He still couldn't bear to mothball the last remnant of the most unforgettable years of his life. Wistfully, he hung the uniform back up in the closet.

He had almost finished and was putting the boxes of old clothes back on the upper shelf where he had found them, after deciding there was no more suitable place in the house to keep them, when he noticed a small black wooden box that he had overlooked before. It was back in the farthermost, darkest corner of the closet. The moment his eye spotted the box, he knew what was inside. He had searched for it many times right after he first came back from Okinawa and had finally decided it was lost forever.

He pulled the black box down, trying to swallow away the excitement in his throat. He lifted the lid gingerly and there it was; the magatama! He held it up and carried it over to the window, fondling its iridescent richness with his fingers as the sunlight danced on the bright emerald-green and black gem and attached silver chain. It was real! It had been lost so long he had almost decided it was something he had imagined. But no, it was real, just like Higa who had given it to him. His mind instantly flashed back to Okinawa, her face, her body, the cove beside the raging surf where they met so many times.

"Oh, Higa, Higa," he said, aloud. "You are real just like this magatama."

He let the shimmering treasure balance on his fingers, then lifted it up, holding onto the chain so the polished stone dangled below, its hues flirting with his eyes.

"How could I have ever lost you?"

His mind searched back. It must have been that summer before he started to medical school that he put the magatama away. During the three years since then, with the years of studies and his days with Anna, he forgot where he put it. He secretly admitted that he had almost forgotten Higa, too, at times, but never completely.

Seeing the magatama now was almost like seeing Higa again. Her warm memories flowed through him—her sweet gentleness and full red lips that tugged alluringly down at the corners when she smiled. Carefully and impulsively, he put the necklace in his pocket and walked out of his room. It was as though his feet were being propelled by some strength alien to his own. He wanted to get away from the droning noise of Harriett's sweeper, to get out into the open where he could think more clearly of Higa.

His steps led him to the windmill, the highest point on the Hawk Ranch. He had climbed it many times as a boy, usually when he wanted to be alone, to dream, to think of things he would do someday, to ponder such things as happiness and freedom and love.

At the top of the windmill, Tom stood up on the platform and grasped the steel frame of the tail section. He was out of breath from the long climb, and he smiled to think how much higher that platform had seemed as a boy.

Higa would have liked the view from the windmill—the vast sea of wheat surrounding the ranch, as far as a person could see, swathed by the wind in ceaseless motion, waving carefree and wild. In a strange way, at that moment, the vast fields of golden grain reminded him of the white-caps of the China Sea off Okinawa that he had watched so many times with Higa. Tom shaded his eyes with his hand so he could see more clearly.

6

Higa's waka came back to Tom as clear as the day she taught it to him on the windy crag perched high above the waves of the China Sea that splashed and romped against Okinawa's western shore:

Waves be still
And quiet wind;
The Deep and Endless
Waits to speak!

Tom could still see her full young lips forming the words as she spoke slowly in a hushed, reverent tone. He would repeat each phrase, trying for the exact same inflections she had given it. The meaning of the waka was not completely clear to Tom but there was something about it that drew their minds together in common understanding. That was why he liked it. And that was why he liked Higa, even from the first moment he was with her. She was as intangible as a spirit, yet so touchable, so warm, so full of life.

Higa was beautiful and voluptuous. There was a freshness about her, a purity in her lithe body like a new wind far out at sea that had never touched anything but the clean surface of the waves. That purity and freshness set her apart from the other Okinawans.

Most of her countrymen were drawn and frightened people who had been caught in the guile and fear of two foreign races that ground each other and their hosts into the bits of death and misery that was Okinawa in World War II. The yellow soldiers sought to hold their arbitrarily-possessed island with suicidal stubbornness, and the Americans fought savagely for the land, inch by inch, with a determined bravery born of a sense of justice and an even deeper belief that their cause was righteous.

Pemeku Higa belonged to this remote mixture of yellow and white people on the "Pearl of the Pacific" known to many as the "land of the happy immortals." Though World War II was not the first incident to disprove this legend, the Okinawans seemed unable to grasp the meaning of the tragic circumstances forced upon them by its after-effects. Their happy dispositions were degenerated to the point of despair in most cases as they wandered about the island trying to salvage remnants of their pre-battle belongings.

Higa was all alone the day Tom first saw her. It was a Sunday afternoon—a bright August day between rains. The humidity hung on Tom heavily. Tramping up and down the mostly deserted hillsides, searching for souvenirs had left him sweaty and spent. The family burial caves, so prevalent in the Okinawan hills, had provided the occupying American soldiers with excellent hunting grounds for souvenirs, yet by the time Tom had arrived for duty, most of the caves had already been ransacked and items of value were not easily found. Tom had hoped to find some small glimmering gem among the ashes of the burial urns that he could take back to Anna.

He entered one of these tombs when he first saw Higa. She was kneeling off to one side of the entrance, apparently praying. It startled Tom momentarily, despite the serenity of what he saw. Her lips moved but she made no sound. She was bent so low in her prayerful attitude that she hadn't seen Tom approach.

Tom stood motionless for a moment as he watched her, contemplating the possibility that this cave he was about to enter probably held the bones of this pretty young girl's ancestors.

He sat down silently, reverently, on a rock at the cave's entrance and waited. He laid his M1 carbine across his lap, wondering if the young girl, surely not over eighteen, might be some kind of a trap. His division had lost twelve men in the past three weeks in "cave incidents."

The war had effectively ended at 8:16 a.m. on August 6, 1945, the moment when Paul Tibbets and the crew of the Enola Gay dropped an atomic bomb on Hiroshima, yet for Tom and his fellow soldiers in the Okinawan hills, the fighting continued sporadically. Japanese soldiers still hid in the caves. Heads of the American souvenir hunters made fine targets when they were silhouetted in the caves' entrances. Therefore, Tom eyed the length and depth of the cave warily.

He waited for the girl to finish praying, and as he watched her, he suddenly became aware that rummaging through the bones of this girl's ancestors would be sheer sacrilege to her—if she were really praying to those ancestors.

Her prayers seemed very genuine, and he sat mesmerized as she stayed for quite a while with her knees on the stony ground. He dug into his shirt pocket for a D-ration chocolate bar and began unwrapping it. In doing so, his carbine fell from his lap and clattered noisily to the ground. The kneeling girl straightened up and arose gracefully to her feet, staring at him, wide-eyed, but seemingly unalarmed.

Tom walked over to her and was surprised when she made no move to run away. Most of the Okinawan girls had been very skittish up to this point, but this one held her ground. He reached out to her with the still unwrapped chocolate bar and said, "You like sweets?"

"Yes, thank you." She smiled gratefully, her black eyes sparkling. She wore a kimono of basa, tattered in places but covering her adequately. It appeared to have been washed very recently. An exotic, intoxicating scent of exquisite wild flowers filled the air around her. She didn't look as hungry or desperate as most of her countrymen. Her black, shiny hair was drawn neatly into a katakashira that barely reached Tom's shoulder.

"I pray for food for my people," she said after studying the chocolate bar for a moment. "Now we have food!"

Technically, the U.S. Army field ration D-bar was food, but it wasn't great food. It was also intended exclusively for survival, so the 4-ounce bars made by the Hershey Company back in the States had been given instructions that it not taste like a real Hershey bar for fear the soldiers would eat them as candy, rather than carrying them until an emergency arose. He smiled at the thought.

"You speak English!" Tom said, amazed at the charm in this waif of a girl.

"Oh, yes. We have schools in Okinawa." She bristled slightly.

"I didn't mean anything bad," Tom stammered. "I just thought most of your people spoke Japanese."

"Most do speak Japanese," she said, smiling and tucking the chocolate bar inside her kimono.

It was then that Tom decided the unique thing about her attractiveness was the way her lips tugged down at the corners of her mouth when she smiled.

"Do you come here often?" he asked.

"Yes—every day." She turned and looked at the late afternoon sun. "I must go now. My father will be waiting." She looked up at Tom with her lips tugged down in a smile.

"Don't leave yet—can't you stay just a little longer? It's been so long since I've talked to a pretty girl." Tom felt his cheeks reddening as he blurted out the words.

Still, he instantly detected a pleased look in her eyes as she turned to look directly in his eyes and smile.

"Besides," he quickly continued, hoping to keep the conversation going, "you didn't tell me your name. Mine's Tom Bristow."

"My name is Higa," she said, a look of amusement flooding her eyes and lips. She leaned back slightly and laughed aloud as she looked steadily up at him. Then with feigned sadness asked, her lips turned downward, "Are you a lonely soldier, Tom?"

"Yes, Higa." He stumbled over pronouncing her name. "How do you say it, H-i-g-a?"

"Yes, HI-guh."

"Higa, that's pretty." He paused for a moment, rolling the name over on his tongue. She started to walk away again and Tom followed her. "Yes, I'm lonely, Higa. I need you to stay and keep me company."

"My father's waiting for me in Shuri." Her black eyes were increasingly filled with amusement.

"Goodbye, Tom," she said, glancing back at him over her shoulder as she walked quickly away. She disappeared in a flowing motion into a mixture of banyan trees and bougainvillea vines toward the south, toward Shuri. Tom climbed up to the top of the hill that Higa had prayed over and tried to catch a glimpse of her but there was nothing to see but green hills and red splashes of bougainvillea and an occasional dash of delicate, pink hibiscus.

It was as though she had never been there at all and Tom wondered why he cared. He had seen thousands of Okinawan women during his two months on the island before he saw Higa. They had all looked alike and had all seemed as inconsequential as the island on which they lived.

But Higa was different. Perhaps it was her unexpected cleanliness, a sort of divine cleanliness, that made her different from the other Okinawan women. Or maybe it was her smile that turned down at the corners of her mouth in an alluring tug or perhaps it was that she was a young woman with the fleshly, universal attraction all young women held over all young men. Whatever it was, Tom liked it.

"I'll have to tell the fellows back at camp about her," he thought, then immediately decided against it. They wouldn't believe him in the first place. Besides that, they would be after her themselves.

It was nearly sundown and Tom had forgotten all about hunting for souvenirs. From the top of Higa's hill he could see the China Sea tossing its white caps against the sun-bronzed shoreline. Perhaps he had found something much better than a souvenir. A feeling of exhilaration coursed through him as he savored in his mind his anticipated meeting with Higa the next day. He would then learn more about this bit of feminine mystery who had seemed so inconsonant with her mundane surroundings.

Higa was there the next afternoon as she had said she would be, but it was clear she was there to "pray for food for her people," not just to meet Tom. Still, she turned quickly this time when Tom approached her and took a flowing step toward him with that smile that tugged at the corners of her mouth so bewitchingly. There was that same wild-flower scent about her and her black eyes danced with the same vigor. Her dress was the same, too, except it had been freshly laundered.

"I hope I didn't interrupt your prayers before you were through," Tom said, hesitantly.

"No, it's all right." She looked waspish standing up beside him. She must have been a good fourteen inches shorter than his six feet-two inches.

"Did you pray for food again?"

"Yes. And it will come," she said confidently.

Tom smiled at her and motioned her to sit with him on the large, smooth rock he had used the day before by the cave's entrance.

"Please be seated, my beautiful princess," he said with a mock bow and a sweep of his hand, "and your prayers will be answered." With that, he took off his field pack and commenced pulling from it cans of C-ration meats, puddings, candies and a couple of cans of pineapple juice given to him by a mess sergeant's aide. He set the goodies on paper napkins spread over the rock beside Higa.

"A feast for a lady," he said, setting the last part of the food in place with a flourish. "Oh, I almost forgot the desert," he added, reaching into his shirt pocket and pulling forth a D-ration chocolate bar.

Higa watched almost in awe as Tom displayed the food. When he had finished, her face broke into a beaming smile and she clapped her hands appreciatively. She offered to help open the cans but Tom said, "No-no, Higa. This dinner's on me, service and all. You just sit there like a lady, and before you know it the feast will commence."

Later, during the meal, Higa became inquisitive and before they had come to the chocolate bar, Tom found himself drawn into telling her about Anna and the Hawk Ranch. Higa sat with her legs under her while Tom leaned back against the rock, his lanky legs stretched out in front of him. Higa ate with a petite-ness that enthralled Tom.

"You're staring at me," Higa said, nibbling at a C-ration biscuit.

"I'm sorry, Higa. I was just thinking how it seems like I've known you all my life. Did you by any chance grow up in Oklahoma?" She laughed with him.

"Oklahoma—Okinawa, they sound alike," she giggled with the most beautiful-sounding laugh he had ever heard. "Do they look alike?"

"Not really. Okinawa has more hills and forests. Oklahoma has no oceans all around. Both places have red dirt though." He looked away from the contours of her small, firm breasts pressed tightly against her kimono, fearing she would accuse him of staring at her again. Despite his best intentions, his gaze returned again and again to her enticing shapeliness.

After eating, they walked to the top of the hill that Tom had stood on the evening before, the hill that Higa considered home to her ancestors' spirits. Once during the climb to the top, Higa grabbed Tom's arm with both hands to steady herself. Her touch filled him with an electric thrill, and he took her hand quickly in his, climbing slowly to permit her to keep pace. She allowed her hand to remain in his even after they reached the top of the hill and they had settled themselves comfortably against the rocks to watch the sea. Just being that close to her, their hands entwined, electrified and amplified deep feelings he had never experienced before.

Waves be still
And quiet wind;
The Deep and Endless
Waits to speak!

She whispered the words to him in a rhythmic reverence that blended into the waves and rocks about them and Tom could hardly determine whether they came from her lips or the wind, or whether they came from her soul or the sea.

The green hills around them caught the brilliant afternoon sun and accentuated the lavish red of the bougainvillea, wild cannas and hibiscus. Even in the midst of a tropical battleground, life continued to burst colorfully from the blood-stained soil.

Okinawa itself, it seemed to Tom, was such an ironic

isle of contrasts. There was so much conflict, from the pounding, rushing feet of soldiers bent on blood-letting to the wholesale death and destruction so foreign to the happy immortal natives.

The one constant was the sea with its incessant swish-swashing, its endless tossing, rolling and rushing toward the rock shore, then back out again. It was entertaining to see, but it was also awe-inspiring. He loved being near such a magnificent sight, smelling its briny odors, hearing the roaring surf and watching its churning ridges break on the rocks.

Was it the sea that thrilled him so? Or was it Higa holding his hand? He wasn't sure, yet somehow it seemed certain that time and tide would someday reveal what he was feeling so passionately and deeply.

The last days of the Okinawan summer wore on for the victorious American soldiers. It, with its frequent rains that splashed unrelentingly against pup tents and helmets, brought a mixture of unrest and anticipation as the men waited with nothing to do but dream of what lay ahead for them now that the war had ended, hoping that their division's eighteen months of active duty in the Pacific had entitled them to go back to the States.

There were fewer and fewer armed skirmishes with Japanese soldiers, so the GIs wrote letters, hunted souvenirs and waited. Okinawa was merely a holding place until the peace treaty with Japan could be signed. Discipline was relaxed and work details were cut to a minimum. The kitchen personnel either didn't know or didn't care that Tom was taking food in quantities considerably more sizeable than was required for one American soldier. He became more and more adept at getting large amounts of food into his field pack and duffle bag without arousing suspicion. He shook off his first few qualms about taking the food by rationalizing that the amount of food he could carry to Higa and her people in his one-man operation would never offset the misery and suffering that the Okinawans had undergone as a result of the uninvited war fought on their island.

Tom never heard Higa complain about the effects of the war, neither for her or her fellow Okinawans, but the results were obvious in a casual glance at the crumbled remnants of the buildings of Shuri and Naha, at the unsealed and ransacked tombs and the destitute looks in the eyes of the skittering little brown people as they searched furtively for food in the untilled land and sought to reclaim homes or possessions that too often no longer existed. The Okinawans also searched, often in vain, for children who had disappeared in the midst of battles that had raged throughout the island.

Higa always smiled and thanked Tom for the food he brought her. He never met any of her family or neighbors, except a wiry little man who started coming with her to help carry the food. She called him Hainju.

"He's like running water," she said, "don't you think? That's what his name means."

Hainju was not related to Higa, but he had been employed by her father so long it seemed he was almost a part of the family. He ran with jaunty steps wherever he went, and he was as tireless and brawny as barbed wire.

Hainju would meet them at the same foot-bridge each evening with a wheelbarrow. With quick, anxious movements he would load his wheelbarrow without saying a word. Tom never knew if Hainju spoke English or not, since the small, sinewy man was always so busy piling the food into the wheelbarrow or pushing the load down the path between the banyan trees. His features were set stoically, and his manner was determinedly non-conversational. Tom never even attempted to speak to him, feeling as if he would be intruding by doing so. With Hainju, talking seemed unnecessary. His eyes spoke volumes, and he seemed grateful for what Tom was doing for his people.

Tom watched the skinny Hainju, as he had so many times before, as the man piled the wheelbarrow high with canned turkey, beans, apple sauce and several sacks of flour and sugar. It was loaded in short order and Hainju pushed it off down the narrow path through the trees toward Shuri. His lean arms and legs pumped rhythmically and his head bent forward over the wheelbarrow and its burden in a union of balance and strength.

"Let's follow him, Higa," Tom said, reaching for her hand. "I've been thinking it would be interesting to see how he distributes the food among 'your people'."

"We can't go now. I haven't said my prayers yet." She gave him a prim little smile and without further ceremony, she dropped to her knees and, bowing her head, commenced praying.

Tom eased over to "their" rock and sat down, hoping she wouldn't be in too much of a spiritual fervor this time, for it was very hot and muggy, and he wanted to know more about her and her people.

It had been raining an hour ago when he left camp and now the sun was out as bright and hot as though there had been no clouds for weeks. Tom watched her and wished he could participate in the prayer with her. With her eyes closed as they were now, it looked like her long lashes covered half of her cheeks. Her kimono hung down loosely from the front of her body as she leaned over. Her legs stuck out behind her from the knees down, flattened against the ground, the calves smooth and well formed. Even her feet were perfect. He felt as if he were gazing at a priceless Gauguin portrait like the ones he had seen in the St. Louis Art Museum during a visit with his father.

Tom had long since lost his sense of intrusion that he had felt that first day when he stumbled upon her during her praying session. He no longer felt embarrassed; rather, he was beginning to feel like he belonged with Higa as she prayed, as though he were somehow an essential part of her prayers. He loved to watch her. She was dedicated to what she was doing, so innocent and pure in appearance, that Tom found himself wanting more and more to share her tranquility, her peace, her faith or whatever it was she had.

Higa prayed on and on, so long that clouds eventually formed again. Typical of the tropical island, the skies began raining large drops on them before Higa could get off her knees.

"I know a place we can go to keep dry,' she said, moving over to Tom and grabbing his hand. "It's nearby. Come, I'll show you the way."

Tom ran with her along the same path Hainju had taken. He hoped she was taking him home with her so he could finally meet her people, but that was several miles away, and they would be soaked by then. The clouds were so heavy it was almost dark. Miraculously, neither of them fell on the slippery footing of the rain-soaked path. Higa's small warm hand was surprisingly strong as she pulled him along, together racing through the wet branches like wild deer. He was relieved when she finally stopped running and, bending low, led him under an ancient wooden bridge that spanned a small stream. It took Tom a few moments to catch his breath before he could speak.

"You came under this bridge like you had been here before," he said, between aching breaths.

"I used to come here as a child and watch the rain splash into the brook like it does now." She glanced about at the tree lined and grassy-banked brook and said, "Isn't it beautiful?"

Tom put his arm about her waist and felt the warm, lithe body moving as she panted from the trek. She looked at him, smiling, her eyes filled with a sort of divine devilishness. The veins in her throat throbbed in and out, and he knew it wasn't altogether the exertion in running to get out of the rain. He pulled her up closer to him and was thrilled when he felt her arms go around his shoulders. She was like a porcelain doll in appearance, but was so much more, so warm and alive.

He wondered what kind of a love he had for this divine creature. It was not the same as the love he had for Anna. He loosened his hold on her at the thought of Anna and she pulled away from him. She stared at the rippling stream for a moment, then commenced repeating the lines of her waka.

Waves be still
And quiet wind;
The Deep and Endless
Waits to speak!

It was not a platonic love, he knew that. Nor was it purely a love of passion, he decided. Still, it was real, as genuine as anything he had ever experienced. It was something that had grown between them that had to be pursued. It was not something he could take off like a garment. It was within him, a part of him now. He couldn't touch it, burn it or dilute it. There was no way to expunge it.

"Forgive me, Anna," he prayed in the only way he knew how.

August ended and Tom had still told no one at camp about Higa. As he continued to take more food at more frequent intervals, he became a little concerned at what might happen if his acts of generosity were traced back to him. Still he never once considered slackening the pace. In fact, he worked at night carrying food from the kitchen to a hiding place near the footbridge where Hainju picked it up.

The news the Americans had been waiting to hear finally came on the morning of September 2, 1945, with Japan's formal surrender that took place on board the battleship USS Missouri, anchored with other United States' and British ships in Tokyo Bay.

Tom and his fellow soldiers would soon be moved to Japan. Though they had known it was coming, the news was met with a great deal of celebrating and hearty "hoo-raws." The men were tired of their dusty, fruitless search through tombs that yielded nothing but the shiny bones of "happy immortals" who once lived on the "Pearl of the Pacific," people who had never known the luxuries of strawberry sodas or white enameled refrigerators, people who had never experienced the pleasure of a five-course dinner at a plush country club. The "happy immortals" had never felt the feeling a business man gets when riding up an elevator twenty-seven floors to a glass-and-walnut suite of offices where he is a respected leader, nor had they ever known the enjoyment of riding seventy miles an hour on a four-lane, asphalt highway. These little brown people lived much like they had existed century after century. Most of the Americans couldn't wait to get back to civilization.

Within a week, orders were cut and posted which assigned some of the men to occupy Japan and allowed others to return to the States for discharge. Tom was in the latter group.

He worked his way out of the group of hilarious soldiers encircling the bulletin board outside the CO's tent. He should have been excited, too, for he had spent many months dreaming of the moment when he would be told he was going home. He had imagined the time when he would stand on board the ship and watch the greenery of the small Pacific island slip away. Sure, he might recall Okinawa from time to time as he talked with chums or family. Maybe he would share the memories with Anna someday, their children or grandchildren.

Now that the time had come, Tom had difficulty believing it was true. He wanted to tell himself that Higa was some sort of a temporal delusion and that he could soon put her out of his mind, that she would leave him, and he would forget her just as soon as he left Okinawa. That is what he hoped as he headed back to the States, to the Oklahoma Panhandle and to Anna Taylor.

As with any graduation, leaving the South Pacific island and Higa caused a bittersweet blend of happiness, fulfillment and unexplainable pangs of misgiving which flooded his heart.

That evening, just as the sun was going down, Tom hurried along the foot-path that he had worn smooth going back and forth from the bivouac area to meet with Higa. Just before he reached Higa's hill, the path forked, one leading southward to later join the path used by Hainju and his wheelbarrow food route and the other leading to Higa's meeting place. Banyan trees and tangles of honeysuckle lined the path and snagged at Tom's fatigue jacket as he sped along. The fragrance of their blossoms flirted with him and, at another time, would have slowed his pace. But tonight Higa was waiting for him and he must hurry. Even the blue-hazed mountains that were visible occasionally through the trees had no fascination for him this evening.

She was there as he knew she would be. She stood by the cave's entrance and Tom knew from the look of concern on her face that she sensed the information he had received earlier. Perhaps she already knew that this was their last day together.

"What kept you, Tom. You're late," she said, running to meet him. She was wearing a new basa kimono, mostly white with only a few pleasingly scattered touches of orange. She was breathtakingly beautiful.

"They kept us busy all afternoon getting us ready to leave."

Tom hadn't meant to blurt out the news quite so abruptly, and her eyes grew tense, misting.

"Your dress is lovely," he tried to gloss over the pain both already knew. "Let me feel to see if it's felt." He laughed at his own trite humor as he put one arm around her and felt the sleeve of her dress with the other hand.

"I knew it would happen," she said, ignoring his attempts to cheer her. "I knew you would leave me. You want to go back to your Anna." Her voice had a mildly bitter ring to it, and her face was suddenly grim.

Tom didn't reply at once. He turned and led her up the side of the hill to the high rock atop her ancestor's cave where they had sat together so many times watching the sea. The sun had set now but darkness was warded off by a bright moon. The smell of honeysuckle wafted its way up to them from the wooded areas below. From their vantage point the hibiscus, cannas and bougainvillea, and even the sea itself blended together into purple-grey velvet in the evening haze. They were all alone in the wrinkles of a lush horizon-to-horizon carpet.

They sat for some time holding each other close, feeling the nearness of each other's heart. In the grey mist, they seemed closer together than they had ever been.

Higa finally broke the silence between them: "I have asked Shineri-kyu to watch over you and bring you safely back to me very soon," She spoke confidently, the concern gone from her eyes.

"Some day I'll come back, Higa—someday." He felt her heart beat faster against him and he held her tighter. "I'll want to come back when I can, because I think I've fallen in love with you."

"I prayed for that, too," she said, her face brightening.

"You mean you asked Shin-n-ner Ku, how did you say it, that too?"

"Yes. Shineri-kyu," she pronounced it slowly for him.

"Who is Shineri-kyu?" Tom asked, feeling a little jealous of her enthusiasm for him when she spoke of the deity she worshiped.

"In the beginning," she said, "there were two gods. One was Shineri-kyu, and the other was his wife, Amami-kyu. They had three children from a passing wind, two sons and a daughter. One son became the first ruler, one son the father of all the common people and the daughter became the first Noro."

She sat very still as she talked, looking at Tom's face as though watching to see whether he believed what she said.

"What's a Noro?" Tom asked, wondering at the attitude of divine passion that had taken hold of her since she started talking about her Shineri-kyu.

"I'm a Noro!" Higa said. She spoke with pride, almost haughtily and with an air of supreme confidence. "The Amami-kyu is my grandmother and she has given me the secret of immortality. Many rulers have tried to obtain this secret."

"Who were some of these rulers, Higa?" Tom asked, thinking he might bring her back down to earth with some factual information.

"Chin Shih Huang Ti, the first emperor of the Kingdom of Yen who built the Great Wall in China was one. He tried to get the secret from my ancestors for years, but he was an evil man and had no success. Another was Yang Chien, emperor of the Sui dynasty. Also Kublai Khan of Mongolia and man rulers of our own Tenson dynasty."

Tom had known all along that her religious beliefs were quite strange, but it seemed eerie to claim that she was descended from a goddess. It was simply too preposterous. And to claim still further that she had the secret to immortality was totally incredulous.

In her own way, he rationalized, Anna had claimed the same thing. "I have eternal life through Jesus Christ," Anna said adamantly many times. Of course Anna hadn't made a ridiculous claim of being descended from a goddess.

"Why do I have to continually get mixed up with women that want me to believe religious mumbo-jumbo that I cannot accept or understand? Why can't I just find one that wants to have fun, to make love, to enjoy the moments together. How can Higa believe this cave-age voodoo?"

Yet, here she was, sitting beside him holding his hand, apparently of sound mind.

"Higa, you've never lied to me," Tom finally said, "and I want very much to believe you. I've loved you from the moment I first saw you. But I can't believe what you have just told me."

"Don't worry, Tom," Higa spoke softly. "You will believe me someday. All I have told you is true, and when you return to me I will give you the secret to immortality. I have not given it to any man before because they did not love me nor I them."

She paused, almost out of breath from her rapid speech. She had pulled herself free from his arms and was sitting very straight as she spoke.

"You will be the first man to have the secret of immortality, for you love me and I love you."

She looked at him with an intensity that almost frightened him. Almost. She continued: "You must promise me that you will tell no one of our words here tonight, and you must promise to return."

She spoke with such sincerity and zeal. Her eyes pierced him with such intensity that before he realized he was talking, he heard himself saying, "I promise to come back to you, Higa. I will come back and learn of your secret, and I will tell no one what you've told me."

She leaned forward and her soft, warm fingers touched his face. For a moment he thought she was going to kiss him; instead, she slipped a necklace from beneath her kimono and put it into his hands. Its curved, shimmering, greenish and black gem was beautiful beyond words, even in the half-light that surrounded them. She said, "This magatama will seal our promises to each other."

"Thank you, Higa. It's beautiful—and I'll keep it until I see you again." Tom held her hands between his, with the magatama pressed between them. She was so close to him he could see her throat throbbing in and out as it had that rainy day under the bridge.

He pulled her closer to him. She didn't resist. Then like the rush of a massive tsunami breaking against the rocky shore, they melted together. She pushed herself into his arms, opening herself to him, surrendering completely. Both were driven by fervent desire and an overwhelming fear of being separated forever. Their lips met in a wild and hungry kiss born from an uncanny, uncontrollable mix of otherworldly worship and earthy passion. Even as he lost himself in the limitless depths of Higa's ageless soul and eager body, inwardly Tom heard the words to her waka again and again, incessant as the sea's crashing surf:

Waves be still
And quiet wind;
The Deep and Endless
Waits to speak!

7

Tom finished lining up his ball and addressed it, ready to putt. He stroked the ball smoothly. The white spheroid rolled twenty feet on the well-manicured grass to the hole, tettered on the edge of the cup, then dropped in.

He had to hand it to Benjamin. His father had built the finest greens he had seen anywhere into his Hawk Ranch course.

He put his club back in the bag and started for the next tee. The droning sounds of an approaching John Deere combine forced his thoughts away from his golf game for a moment. Like gigantic monsters from a Grade B drive-in movie, the huge harvesting machines, with their unmistakable green skin and yellow markings had been circling around him in the golden wheat fields which adjoined the golf course for the past several days. They hadn't interfered with Tom's game, nor had his thoughts of Higa been disturbed. He had thought of her a lot since finding her magatama a few days before, and those memories had stirred him deeply, unlocking passions and emotions he had almost forgotten.

Tom felt in his pocket for it now and rubbed the slick surface of the green-colored gemstone absentmindedly, even as he watched one of the harvesting machines stop only a hundred yards away from the number eight tee where he was standing.

The chaff-covered, sun-helmeted driver cut off the motor, climbed down from the driver's seat and walked quickly in Tom's direction. By the time the worker had walked twenty yards, Tom could see it was the pudgy-faced Willie Lusby. Tom walked off the edge of the tee a short distance to see what the despised man could possibly want with him.

"How come you're running a combine yourself, Willie?" he heard himself saying casually. "I thought you were supposed to be the boss."

Tom had meant it to be a joke, but the words came out rather caustic. Despite the thick layer of dust and chaff on Willie's face, Tom thought he saw him turn a deeper shade of red.

"Dammit," Willie shouted, standing close to Tom and heaving his heavy waistline in and out with short breaths, "your old man's so tight—all that money he's got stacked away in his safe—and he can't hire me enough good men to get all this wheat in."

Willie paused to catch his breath, then he continued, venomous cynicism hot on his lips, "I came over to see if you'd like to try your hand at runnin' one of these big boys. I thought you might be tired of pussy-footing your way around this here sissy golf course." He squinted challengingly.

"You're asking me to run one of the combines?"

"Yep! You might enjoy working a little around here if you ever tried it."

Willie's voice was a mixture of bitterness and superior disdain. Tom regretted making his provoking remark about being the boss. There was something very vengeful and evil about Willie Lusby that bothered him deeply. Tom could only look past the hulking man and see the vision in Lonnie's Pool Hall with Jennings' helpless, pleading eyes as he croaked, "The score's forty-seven to forty-seven—the score's tied—it's not forty-seven to forty-nine!"

"Frankly," Tom said wanly to Willie, forcing the thoughts of Jennings away from his mind, "I'm not sure my Dad would want me to run one of the combines. That's why he hired guys like you who are supposed to know what they are doing."

There was simply something about Willie that seemed extremely sinister and menacing. Tom knew the bully's ham-hock hands, coated with sweat and grease, could maul him in the same savage way as he did Jennings. Of course, Willie wouldn't dare do it out of fear of losing his job, not until the harvest was over anyway.

"Hoss, if I was in your shoes and had a daddy with the kind of money Mister Bristow has, I'd never work another day in my life," Willie said, looking toward the house enviously. Willie squirted a tobacco-stained stream of saliva toward the number eight tee and said, "You're damned lucky you was born rich, cause you'll never make it on your own. And I still don't see what that preacher's daughter sees in you." With that he turned and started stomping triumphantly back to his combine.

Tom watched Willie's spittal foam and dissipate as it sank into the rich green grass near the number eight tee box. A fury rushed through him. He felt perspiration running down his temples from the band in his cap. He clutched the magatama in his hand.

"Wait a minute," Tom shouted toward Willie. "I don't have a problem running the combine or driving a truck or shoveling grain. I've done things much harder than that. But I think you'd better check with my Dad first."

"Sure, sonny boy," Willie yelled back, sneering derisively. "I'll check with your dear ole Daddy and get back to you."

"What a crude man!" Tom said out loud, noting pointedly that Willie was already out of earshot. He teed up his ball and swung viciously, barely topping the ball, sending the white spheroid bouncing nonchalantly, floundering, then stopping less than twenty yards down the fairway. Red-faced, yet without bothering to see if Willie was watching, Tom walked the few steps to the ball, snatched it up, grabbed his bag of clubs and walked back to the house, mentally kicking himself for allowing Willie's caustic words to bother him so deeply.

Tom had made it a point to avoid Willie Lusby after he came to work on the Hawk Ranch, and he would have avoided Benjamin, too, except Harriett insisted on serving them their meals together. They usually ate in silence, with the older man reading the *Panhandle News-Herald,* leafing through farming and ranching magazines, or poring over a copy of the *Wall Street Journal.* Occasionally he would utter a short outburst at Harriett over some deficiency in the cuisine, imagined or real.

"Heard you wanted to drive one of my combines," Benjamin said the morning after Tom's conversation with Willie at the eighth tee.

"I told Willie I could," Tom tried not to act surprised. "I told him he'd have to talk with you—that I didn't think you wanted me on any of the machinery."

"Where'd you get that idea?" the older man shot back.

"Isn't that pretty much what you always told me around here through the years?" Tom asked. "You didn't even want me to play sports for fear I'd mess up my fingers and destroy my future as a medical doc...."

He tried to stop in mid-sentence, but it was too late. What both of them had carefully, painstakingly tried to avoid was suddenly thrust openly on the table, as real and vivid and obvious as the colorful food on Harriett's breakfast plates. The air inside the dining room thickened and chilled instantly.

Benjamin put down his newspaper and directed an even, steely gaze at his son: "I reckon that doctor thing won't be much of a problem any more, now, will it?"

"I guess not." Tom worked hard to keep the anger from rising in his voice.

"Then I guess it's not a problem for you to get those lily whites of yours dirty doing a man's job out here on the ranch, then will it?"

"I guess not."

"Well," his Dad's voice softened slightly, "you might as well do something worthwhile around her while you figure out whatever the hell it is you want to be. I'll pay you the same as any other hired hand. You decide."

"I've already told Willie I'd drive a combine or a truck or whatever you need, but he'd have to talk with you first."

"We talked," Benjamin breathed with an air of superior finality. "It's damned fine with me. We'll start running the combines this morning as soon as the wheat is dry enough to cut. Show up if you want. Don't show up if you don't want. Just don't expect any money from me anymore if you don't work."

"I don't have a problem working for you," Tom answered. "I can do anything you need around here. I've done tougher in my life. I just didn't want to be in your way."

"You're not in the way," Benjamin spoke with more emotion than he cared to divulge. "It might be nice to have another Bristow working around the Hawk Ranch. I'm tired of all the damned hired hands that just want a paycheck but don't give a fig about the equipment or this place."

He said the word "place" almost reverentially.

With that Benjamin stood and left the room, an obvious signal that the conversation was over. Tom didn't know if he should be relieved that the silence was broken or angry that such an obvious gauntlet had been thrown down.

"Show up if you want," his father had challenged. "Don't show up if you don't want. Just don't expect any money from me if you don't work."

Money!

A plan began to form in Tom's mind.

He had hoped that Benjamin's bitterness over his failure to graduate would disappear eventually, but the chasm between them was too wide to ever be crossed now. It was apparent, as far as his father was concerned, that Tom might as well be tossed into that chasm and buried. The younger Bristow had resolved himself to his fate and knew he had to move on with his life. Working in the harvest and getting paid crew wages was a start as he began figuring out what he wanted to do next.

Tom had heard the story about the combines several times from his father. During the war, short supplies of farm machines and the raw materials to make them, combined with increased demand for food, produced some amazing advances and unique marketing schemes. In the process, an entire new industry was born that directly affected the Hawk Ranch.

All farm equipment manufacturers had to deal with several undeniable factors during the war. Iron and steel were rationed, used almost exclusively to build warships and airplanes. This directly affected farmers as new machinery became extremely scarce. Gasoline, likewise, was rationed for everyone, including farmers. Farming also changed drastically during the early Forties as huge numbers of farmer's sons and farm workers were drafted or volunteered. Others moved to cities and began working at better paying defense industry jobs. Still, even with the rationing and reduced manpower, America desperately needed bountiful harvests from the nation's heartland.

Prior to the attack on Pearl Harbor, the Massey-Harris farm implement corporation started testing its first self-propelled grain combines. Those early models attracted favorable attention, since the machines combined different functions—cutting the grain, as well as threshing or separating the grain from chaff. Prior cutting and threshing machinery had been pulled around the fields by horses and eventually by tractors.

The implement manufacturers asserted that the combine was able to avoid spilling as much grain back onto the ground. Massey-Harris amassed numerous statistics that pointed to greater fuel efficiency, as well. Using these figures, the company put together an ambitious plan and presented their "Harvest Brigade" campaign to the U.S. War Production Board. They asked for enough steel to produce the combines, promising to sell the new machines only to farmers across the nation who would pledge to harvest at least 2,000 acres of wheat with each combine. Not surprisingly, since he had one of the largest farms in the Panhandle, Benjamin Bristow was one of those farmers who were selected.

The plan seemed both practical and patriotic, and the War Board gave the go-ahead. During 1944, Benjamin and 499 other farmers were allowed to order Massey-Ferguson Model 21 combines for $2,500 apiece. Some went out West, but most were delivered to the Great Plains region. Since they had to harvest at least 2,000 acres, many not only used the combines for their own farms, but also contracted with other farmers to harvest their crops more efficiently. The rate for contract harvesting that first year was three bucks an acre.

Benjamin got his first Model 21 in time for the 1945

harvest. From the beginning, the Harvest Brigade was an overwhelming success, made even more popular by newspapers, radio stations, magazines and Movietone newsreels which all publicized this adventuresome campaign.

By the time World War Two ended, Massey-Harris completely dominated the self-propelled combine market. Other companies scurried to catch up. John Deere, as an example, didn't finish developing their inaugural self-propelled combine, the Model 55, until 1947, and Benjamin Bristow, always a loyal Deere tractor owner, was one of the first in the country to get rid of the red Massey-Ferguson harvester and convert to the combines bearing his beloved green and yellow paint. He bought three Model 55 combines at $4,700 each, which he used through his own harvest each year, then he leased them out to a neighboring farmer who ran a custom harvester business the remainder of the summer through Kansas, Colorado, Nebraska, through the Dakotas, and even into southern Canada. Benjamin paid for the combines the very first year through the custom cutter payments.

Tom got a friendly hired hand named Billy to teach him what he needed to know about running the Model 55. By mid-morning, when the wheat was dry enough to begin cutting, he climbed the ladder to the harvester and took the last place behind the other two Deeres. The three machines, each with twelve-foot headers up front, cut an impressive swath.

It wasn't hard work. The land was flat, so there was little danger of digging one end or the other of the platform into the dirt. Mainly he had to make sure that the harvester ran properly and at the right speed to avoid clogging the belts and machinery. Since he was behind two seasoned hired hands, keeping things going was a breeze. Generally the green wheat bins filled up at the same time for all three combines, so the trucks came at the same time to empty each of them.

There was a simple satisfaction Tom felt as he pulled the lever to start the augur pouring wheat from the combine's grain bin up the side spout into the waiting trucks. There was something earthy and rewarding about the process that ended with the finished grain spilling out into the truck beds.

Tom ate lunch with the other crew members every day. Harriett delivered mountains of sandwiches, platefuls of sliced cucumbers and cantelopes, which the workers swilled down with gallons of ice tea. Tom went out of his way to be just another hired hand, not the owner's son, and the rest of the guys seemed to appreciate that. He was mildly amused at the colorful cussing and sexual bragging he heard, not unlike the gabfests that took place during the time he had spent in the military.

Not surprisingly, Willie tried to provoke Tom every chance he could in front of the other workers, calling attention to his soft college-boy hands and tender, sunburned skin, but being the son of a rich farmer had taught him well how to avoid class-envy confrontations. Numerous times in the Guymon schools, at college and even during his time in the army, he had been taunted by a long line of poorer boys who instinctively disliked guys who came from a nicer background. He had developed his peacemaker skills well, honed in the face of fists.

Before long, Willie silently and grudgingly acknowledged that Tom was pulling his own weight. That didn't stop him from trying to provoke the younger Bristow, of course. Unsuccessful with those taunts, he usually turned to make life miserable for other hired hands who had no deflecting skills and weren't the son of the boss.

By the time harvest was completed, Tom knew the freedom he had hoped to find on the Hawk Ranch was not what he was looking for. Dealing with the likes of Willie took skills he disdained and energies he didn't want to exert. Whatever else he did with his life, he didn't want to have to deal with primitive bullies like Willie. Life was too short.

During the long hours, often until dark each day, he drove the third-in-a-row John Deere combine and relished the opportunity to sort out his life. He thought of Anna, precious Anna, so pure and full of hope, so loyal to her family. But she wasn't free.

He thought of Higa, too.

"If there is such an elusive thing as freedom," he told himself, "it had to be with Higa. She has the secret to immortality."

Strange, he reflected, that he should carry this magnificent secret in his head all these years and only now come to know the true value of it. It was like finding a miraculous cure for some dread disease by stumbling on a combination of drugs that had been kicked around underfoot all along.

He even thought of Jeanie, Judge Anson's daughter. He heard that she and her father were planning to visit the Hawk Ranch after harvest was over. She was such a playful vixen. He wondered what life would hold if he ended up with someone as free and fun-loving as Jeanie. She would be fun to make love with, he knew, but would she ever be more than an elusive butterfly, like too much cotton candy as a child at the carnival—inviting to eat, but too much was simply too much? Still, the delicious idea of too much Jeanie was an intriguing, deeply erotic thought.

Soon harvest was over. Tom continued helping as the huge combines were cleaned, serviced, and turned over to the neighboring farmer and his custom harvesters to begin the trek north. Some of the Hawk Ranch crew went along. Others, including Willie, were hired to finish constructing the extra granaries. Tom considered going with the custom harvest crew, but decided against it.

The next morning Tom sat with his father at breakfast in their usual silence. The younger Bristow had worked much harder than anyone could have imagined, Benjamin included, but while the other hired hands had grown to respect Tom, his father didn't even seem to notice or care.

"No problem," Tom thought, "I don't need his approval. If he wants to stay mad about the fact that I quit med school, so it is. I don't care."

The newly-born sun sprayed its red rays on them through the screen door at the east end of the kitchen. Harriett's dogged puttering back and forth cast long shadows across the breakfast table from time to time.

Harriett came with more coffee. Tom watched the steam swirl about in his cup above the black, bubbling, rising surface of the coffee. Her bony arm moved to hover over Benjamin's half-full cup.

"Don't pour me any more," he snapped, looking up from his paper. "I've got to get out and see what that dolt Willie Lusby is doing, if anything. I picked one hell of a foreman this year. Still, I need him to finish up a few things and watch over the hired help putting those new granaries up." The rancher stood up quickly, walked over and took his hat from a peg behind the kitchen door, then he walked outside.

The phone rang and Harriett hurried into the hallway

to answer it.

"It's for you Tom," she said. For some reason she never had trouble hearing the phone ring or talking on it, Tom mused as he went to answer it. She only had trouble with Benjamin's voice when he was cranky. He laughed inwardly at her subtle cleverness.

It was Anna. Her voice sounded so distant as she spoke. "Tom, I wanted to call and tell you about Mother. She passed away during the night."

She gave details about the funeral, but Tom had quit listening. He grasped the receiver in one hand and the magatama in the other. His brain pumped madly trying to hold all the frustrating thoughts that flooded in. Anna was free now! She was free like he was. Like Higa.

He thought of Anna laughing again. Then he quickly pondered Higa, of her promise, her ludicrous but inescapable promise. He imagined Higa on the hill overlooking the Pacific Ocean, hoping and waiting for Tom to return. But mostly, at that moment, his thoughts were of Anna. She had been his first love, his longest love, perhaps his forever love. Perhaps this, at this precise moment, was a providential sign, if such a thing truly existed.

He didn't remember telling Anna goodbye. Without the slightest trace of hesitation, he put the magatama back in the little black box in the closet. His beloved Anna would need him now, and he would have to go to her. He felt a tremor of shame pass through him that he had become so excited over someone's death, but the shame was rapidly dispelled by the new hope mushrooming within him, hope that Anna's love was now free for him to possess and that he would no longer be forced to share his loved one with her mother.

His thoughts were selfish, he knew, but he couldn't stem the dizzying thoughts that flowed freely.

The activities swirling around Mrs. Taylor's funeral gave little time for talking to Anna. Relatives arrived from far away. Members of the family, church and the surrounding community came in droves to say goodbye to the obviously-loved woman. Tom went to the funeral home the night before the funeral, waited through the long procession of mourners, hugged Anna, and shook Dr. Taylor's hand.

The pastor was warm with his greeting, as always, and spoke kindly to him, but Tom's beloved hardly acknowledged him. Anna was grieving, of course, but he instinctively wondered if it were something more. The same thoughts continued to pelt him through the funeral. He decided to wait a day or so before trying to talk with her, allowing friends and family to depart.

At home, Benjamin was so busy with overseeing the construction on the new granaries that he hardly acknowledged Tom was alive. He obviously knew Anna's mother had died. The obituary was in the newspaper and on the Guymon radio station for all to hear. Still, if the rancher knew, he didn't let on, nor did he repeat his threats about taking Tom out of the will if he saw the "preacher's daughter" again. Apparently Mrs. Taylor's death brought an uneasy truce between the younger and elder Bristows. Perhaps. Possibly.

Tom, at this point, didn't totally care what his father thought. If he disowned him for comforting a young woman for whom he cared deeply, then he would just have to be disowned. Tom had to begin living his own life, sooner rather than later.

Dr. Adam Taylor's house stood adjacent to the Guymon Community Church, just two blocks off the city's Main Street. Both structures were clean and well-cared-for, yet both buildings looked drab in comparison to Tom's shiny maroon Ford convertible parked out front.

The church lawn was brown and worn thin in patches, probably by the prancing feet of children as they tugged at their mothers to take them home or as they chased each other about after the Sunday morning services while their parents discussed the sermon or last Friday's ice cream social. Dr. Taylor's lawn, on the other hand, was green and neatly trimmed, well kept like Dr. Taylor himself, Tom thought.

The house looked deserted as Tom approached the front porch. Dr. Taylor was possibly out making calls, and Anna had probably gone shopping.

"Life must go on," Tom thought to himself, "even after death."

After several knocks at the door, he decided he had chosen a bad time to call on the Taylors. Then the door opened. It was Anna. Quickly, she came out on the porch, smiling, yet looking thinner than the last time he had seen her. The brown and yellow cotton dress hung loosely about her waist and her eyes had a rather forlorn, longing look about them. He wasn't sure if she was truly glad to see him or not, but he felt better when she took his hand and pulled him down beside her onto the wide, wooden porch swing that had hung on its flimsy-appearing chains ever since Tom could remember. They had sat together on it countless times together as they worked on homework together or simply discussed the mysteries of life together. It had been that way since their junior year in high school. It had been that way many times since.

"I'm so sorry about your mother," Tom said, wishing he could hurry and get that part of his visit over. He had never known what to say about people dying. Death somehow seemed out of place in the midst of life.

"I tried to talk with you at the funeral home and church, but it never seemed like the right time to tell you what I really wanted to say," he spoke earnestly.

"It's all right, Tom," she said smiling, "I know you were there for me. That's all that mattered."

Breezes blew her hair playfully. The sun's rays shone through her wisps, bringing out the red highlights, turning her beautiful locks into fine-spun gold. The color contrasted sharply with her almost colorless cheeks.

Tom took her hand and looked into her eyes a long time; those gentle brown eyes that he had loved so long, that looked so strangely forlorn now. Her mother's death seemed to weigh even more heavily on her than did her life.

In an effort to cheer her he said, "I've got some exciting plans for us, Anna. I want to get you out of this house—out into the sun. I want to get the color back into your cheeks like it used to be."

He cupped his hand under her chin and looked at the beautiful lines, the softly curving lips, the slightly turned-up nose and the delicately shaped ears. He had almost forgotten how beautiful she really was.

She pulled her face away from his hand and turned her head toward the street. Then Tom heard the tapping of a cane on the sidewalk out front and his irritation subsided when he saw why Anna had pulled away from him so abruptly. An old man was puttering his way down the sidewalk with much assistance from his cane, glancing occasionally at them as he struggled along.

"That's Mr. Jarnigan," she said. "You probably don't know him, but you should. He's the nicest old thing. He's the janitor at the church, and he'll be 82 years old next month. Everyone loves him."

Anna's eyes beamed as she spoke. Tom felt a little jealous that she should give the old man so much attention at this particular moment.

Hoping to get her mind off the old man, Tom suggested that they go out to lunch. At that, she jumped out of the swing and ran to the door. "Oh, my goodness! I almost forgot my meatloaf. It's probably burning. Come on in…" She spoke the last part over her shoulder as she moved quickly through the door and toward the kitchen.

It wasn't burnt. In fact, Dr. Taylor was using gigantic oven mitts to pull the meatloaf out of the oven as the two young people rushed into the kitchen.

"Please have lunch with us," Dr. Taylor said when he saw Tom. He smiled warmly in his quiet, dignified way, pulled off the right oven mitt, and held out his hand. Tom stopped and shook hands firmly with him. They chatted briefly before Anna called them to the table.

Anna divided the steaming meatloaf, then served stewed apples, carrots and hot rolls. Before they started eating they bowed their heads while Anna prayed over the meal.

"Anna said grace for us so well when she was a child that we just never let her quit," Dr. Taylor smiled warmly as they started eating. His explanation was unnecessary, though, as Tom had heard her do it hundreds of times. He remembered she had asked if he wanted to pray before a meal once and how embarrassed he had been. He had quickly declined, and she never asked again.

"Tom, why don't we visit a few moments in my study while Anna is clearing the table?" Dr. Taylor said as they were finishing their rice pudding dessert.

Tom agreed readily and followed him into his study. The room was the same as it had always been except another wall of shelves had been added. The apparently well-read books on each of the walls placed quite orderly, a silent reflection of Dr. Taylor. Tom felt at ease in the study despite what he feared Dr. Taylor wanted to discuss—his failure to complete medical school. Dr. Taylor had always encouraged him in his studies, so Tom braced himself for the coming reprimand.

The old minister moved behind his desk as he motioned Tom to a large leather-upholstered chair. Dr. Taylor continued standing, shuffling papers about on his desk for a moment before speaking. Finally, he looked at Tom with his grey, piercing eyes. For a moment, Tom felt he was being examined, much like another ponderous theological doctrine. He was fearful of what the pastor would say, yet he was anxious for the older man to quit studying him with his piercing stare, to say something, anything, to break the silence.

"Tom," he began, "it has been a long time since you've really visited with me. In fact, I haven't had a down-to-earth talk with you since you were in high school here in Guymon. You've been here a lot to see Anna, and she let me read some of your letters while you were at the University of Oklahoma, overseas in the service and at medical school. Still, I've missed our talks like we had before."

He smiled and continued. "I know how much you and Anna think of each other, and I wish you would bring me up to date on how you've been and what you plan to do now that you've quit your medical studies."

Tom sprawled his legs out in front of him over the shiny linoleum and leaned back in the huge, comfortable chair, relieved that Dr. Taylor had accepted his decision to quit medicine so amicably.

"Well, Dr. Taylor, there isn't much to tell. I've been at the Hawk Ranch this summer. I helped out with harvest, but now it's over, and..."

Tom wasn't sure where to go next. His voice trailed off. He wanted to say that everything had changed now that Anna was free. Actually, as that thought ran through his brain, it suddenly occurred to him that even in the midst of the family's grief, this was also a time of new beginnings. This might be an opportune time to tell Dr. Taylor that he wanted to marry Anna. He had never thought it would be absolutely necessary to ask him, for it had always been understood in Anna's family that he and Anna would someday be married. But somehow, here in the austerity and silence of Dr. Taylor's study, it seemed proper to ask Dr. Taylor for his blessing.

"You remember I asked Anna to marry me once and that we've been waiting ever since—I haven't talked to her about it since Mrs. Taylor's death—but..."

"And you want my blessing?" The old minister pushed his chair back from his desk and stood up. "Is that it, Tom?"

Tom took his eyes off the floor and glanced up at the piercing eyes. "Yes, sir."

Dr. Taylor turned and walked over to the window, staring out at the sun-bright yard for some time, saying nothing. Tom wondered what he was thinking and what his response would be. Maybe he was thinking about Anna and the long years she had spent waiting on her mother. Tom's thought raced to the endless bed pans, sheets to be changed, trips trudging back and forth from the kitchen to the bedroom with trays of food, and the years of waiting.

Dr. Taylor interrupted his thoughts by clearing his throat and saying, "Tom, I've been wanting to talk to you about Anna. She's not..." He turned as Anna came to the doorway, apparently not wanting her to hear what he was going to say.

Anna, drying her hands on her apron, said to her father, "Mr. Harris, the new organist, is here. He wants to ask you some questions about tomorrow morning's service."

Dr. Taylor hesitated, looking first at Anna, then Tom. He left without saying anything more, and Tom followed Anna back to the kitchen. She tossed a tea towel at him and said with a little laugh, "I'm glad Mr. Harris arrived so I could get you out here to help me, you lazy oaf!"

Tom laughed and commenced trying to put the dishes Anna had rinsed into the dishwater. The twinkle in her eyes as she laughed was more like his old Anna.

"You know," he spoke warmly, "I'd rather be here slaving over these dishes than in there talking with your father anyway."

"Oh, you don't like my father?" She raised her eyebrows pretending to be hurt.

"You know I didn't mean that," he said and then they both laughed again.

After a moment of listening to the comforting sounds of dishes clanking softly against each other in the dishwater, Tom said, "You know, even the way you wash dishes makes me love you more."

Anna looked up at him questioningly, resting her hands for a moment on the edge of the sink.

"What I mean," Tom added, "is that you handle each dish as though it were one of the few left in the world, as if it had to be so clean it could be showcased at the county fair."

She smiled, showing teeth that were straight, white, and beautiful. Then her face sobered and she said, "Maybe it's because this is one of the few things I know how to do well, or maybe it's..." she paused, as though pondering the matter for the first time, "or maybe it's because I love the people that ate out of them."

Tom dried off his hands, pulled her away from the sink and dried her hands with the tea towel she had given him.

"Maybe it's because you're so full of love that it spills out on everything you touch," he said. Her eyes filled with that forlorn look that he had noticed before lunch. He pulled her close against himself.

"I wish you could love me like that," he said. "I wish I could be one of your shiny dishes." He smoothed at a curl that stuck out stubbornly away from her temple.

Then he kissed her. At that moment she seemed as if she were the only girl he would ever truly love. However, even before the kiss ended, he felt her pulling away from him. She turned and leaned over the sink. She began sobbing, quietly at first, then gradually with long, unrestrained sobs.

Tom placed his arm around her, leaned down beside her and kissed her tear-drenched cheek.

"I hurt for you, Anna," he said softly. "I understand. I lost a mother, too, remember?" He felt tears in his own eyes as he spoke.

He waited, trying to force the sobbing to stop with the pressure of his hands against her shaking body. Finally, she became quiet, dried her eyes on her apron and said, "I'm sorry. It's not just my precious mother. Tom, I can't explain why I'm crying. It's been so long since we've been together like this." Her eyes brightened and she smiled. "Would you still want to take me for a ride in your new car?"

"Sure—sure. I'll finish up the dishes while you go freshen up. Run on, now," Tom said, giving her a slight nudge. He went back to the sink wondering what had brought on the outburst of crying. He also wondered why she had suddenly decided to go for a ride in the convertible.

He was simply glad to see that she was no longer weeping.

"No man knows how to handle a woman crying," he thought, "certainly not me."

She had always been strong and cheerful. Anna was always the encourager and comforter. But something seemed so different.

The sun was still high in the late July afternoon

when they left the house. They walked leisurely down the front walk toward Tom's car. Anna's face showed no trace of tears now as she stayed close beside him, calm and relaxed. She had changed into a soft green dress that enhanced and deepened the brown in her eyes.

"Your new car is a beauty, Tom," Anna said admiringly as they approached it. And its clean maroon lines, accented by shimmering chrome, were indeed resplendent in the bright sunlight.

Tom had already opened the car door for Anna to enter when she suddenly straightened and, looking at the church, said, "Oh, Mr Jarnigan must have forgotten to close the church door. He's getting a little absent-minded lately." She looked at Tom apologetically. "If you don't mind, Tom, we had better go shut it."

Tom led the way across the thin, worn grass of the church yard and was in the process of closing the door when Anna said, "Maybe we'd better look inside to see if Mr. Jarnigan might still be working before we shut it. He's usually through by noon on Saturdays, but he might have found some extra chores to do."

They went through the opened side door facing the Taylor parsonage. It led directly into the basement of the church which was used as a recreation room for Boy Scouts, dinners and other activities. The room was filled with chairs and tables and was very still, with the vacuum stillness that only churches on Saturday afternoons can have. It was so dark that Tom and Anna had difficulty finding their way through the maze of chairs and tables to the stairway leading up to the main sanctuary on the ground floor. Occasionally they would bump into a chair, and the scraping of the chair leg across the concrete floor would resound about them in the huge stillness like unexpected thunder.

They said nothing as they peered briefly into the darkened choir-robe room and four small class rooms. The cracking of their heels sounded like rifle shots as they climbed the concrete stairway to the main floor. It was obvious that Mr. Jarnigan was not in the church. They stood together at the rear of the sanctuary looking at the empty pews. The stained glass windows threw brilliant patterns of color on the rows of empty seats, guilding some of the tattered hymnals which attested to Mr. Jarnigan's workmanship by standing very erect in their proper places.

The silence was immense. Tom had been in only a few churches in his lifetime and in this particular church only twice—once with Anna during Thanksgiving vacation when he returned from Okinawa and most recently at Mrs. Taylor's funeral. Then, it had seemed like any other church—people dressed up, dignified, coughing, reading, singing, praying. He remembered looking around during the prayers. Some sat with eyes open, looking straight ahead, but most had their eyes shut and heads bowed. It was such a foreign world to him.

He remembered after the Thanksgiving service how people rustled about, saying "come over for dinner," "fine sermon, wasn't it?" and patting little boys on the head as the youngsters struggled with stiff shirts and scratchy wool trousers.

Tom thought of the contrast. It was different now, more like a church should be; a quiet peaceful place where there was ample room for thinking, where one could hope and love. Yes, this would be a good place for love to live and grow. He wondered if Anna thought the same thing. From the glow in her eyes, he felt certain she was. He put his arm around her waist and pulled her close to him. She leaned her head against his shoulder and said nothing, continuing to look at the empty pews, the stained glass windows with their brilliant reds, blues, oranges, yellows, purples, greens splashing over the sun-glossed lectern.

"You know something, Anna?" He was almost frightened at the hugeness of his own voice as it reverberated about in the surrounding stillness. He spoke more softly, "You know, Anna, this would be a wonderful place for a wedding." He smiled down at her but she didn't return his smile; she kept looking straight ahead.

After a moment, she answered, "Yes, I've been to lots of weddings here. They are always lovely."

She was being unnecessarily objective, Tom thought. Maybe she was doing it purposefully, as if trying to see what he would say next.

He cupped his hand under her chin and turned her face up to his. "Let's get married right away—let's get married this week! We can go to Mexico for our honeymoon or wherever you want."

He didn't have all the money he needed for such an impulsive promise, but he could get it from Benjamin. He could borrow it from a bank. He could...

Tom watched Anna's eyes, expecting them to brighten with enthusiasm to match his own. He expected them to shine with anticipation and to feel her heart beat faster against him as he held her close. Instead, she turned and stared at the lectern again. He turned her loose, a flood of anger surging through him. Surely, she couldn't still be letting her mother stand in their way. True, it had been a very short time since her death, but it hadn't been sudden or unexpected, and they had looked forward to Anna being free to marry for such a long, long time. How could she reject him now?

He looked at her sad, forlorn eyes and he could feel her slipping away as though an icy hand had come between their hearts and was silently, forcefully tugging at her, pulling her away from him.

"Anna—Anna—we've waited and hoped so many years. Have all those years of hoping died? Please don't just ignore me, Anna. I love you too much to lose you now. I need you."

He felt hot, furious tears spilling out over his eyelids into rivulets on his face. His words seemed to fall only on empty pews. It was as though the shaft of sunlight slanting down on the lectern held Anna captive and made it impossible for her to yield to his pleadings or the pulling motions of his hands on her arms.

"I'm sorry, Tom," she said, turning her face up to his. She blinked the tears from her eyes and her voice quavered as she spoke. "Maybe it's just as well that we discuss it right away like this. You might as well know now. I can't marry you. I can't tell you everything, and I ...I love you. Still, I can't marry you!"

She threw herself against him and sobbed against his chest, her whole body racked and shaking as though her heart were breaking.

"Why, Anna? Why? Why in God's name can't you? This is what we've both been living for all our lives. You know that. Why can't you marry me?"

Anna pulled away from him and walked a few steps down the isle toward the lectern. Then she turned and ran back to him and threw her arms about his shoulders and kissed him with a fervor that Tom had never known could exist. It was as if her passion had been caged up inside her heart all these long years and had just now been unloosed. She kissed him again and again as the tears ran down her face.

Then, as suddenly as she had run to him, she twisted away from his arms and ran to the door. She stopped, and facing him again and raising her hand in a hesitant, half-waving gesture, she said, "I love you, Tom. I just can't marry you. It's too late! Goodbye, Tom. You have to move on with your life. Goodbye!"

She gasped back a sob and disappeared down the steps. Tom rushed to the door and got there just in time to get a glimpse of the hem of her green dress as she flung herself through the front door into the parsonage.

He wanted to run after her, to force her to be logical. He wanted her to explain.

"How could it be too late? How could she love him, yet not want to marry him?"

Nothing made sense anymore.

Tom's convertible hummed furiously over the asphalt highway from Guymon to the Hawk Ranch with a incessant rhythm that would have put him to sleep were it not for the furious remorse that hammered away inside him.

Her words tormented him: "I love you, Tom. I just can't marry you. It's too late! Goodbye, Tom!"

Goodbye? How could it be goodbye, just like that.

He was furious. He was lost. He was defeated. He was jealous of whatever or whomever was causing the breach between Anna and him. He was even angry at God for whatever role He played in the utter destruction of his heart.

He had lost her. Was it his lack of direction, especially in comparison to her father's steady determination? Could it be that she had sensed his feelings for Higa—that somehow Higa's secret, her secret of immortality had risen up between them. Or perhaps with her keen woman's intuition she had seen his lustful thoughts about Jeanie?

None of those thoughts made any sense. Nothing did.

The long black road back to the Hawk Ranch split the yellow wheat stubble in half, stretching on both sides and ending only at the horizon. Here and there a tractor crawled stubbornly along, leaving behind a spiraling plume of dust and chaff, bouncing sharply now and then as though to shake off the burdensome plow, yet with no success.

"I love you, Tom. I just can't marry you. It's too late! Goodbye, Tom!"

Anna's words continued to hammer at him, hanging to his thoughts tenaciously like the plow behind the tractor.

"Maybe love is always like the wheat," Tom's thoughts ran zigzagged through his brain, making little sense, seeking little sense. "Maybe it always starts out like a fresh new wheat plant, full of tender green life, yet bending to the wind and accepting the scorching midday heat along with the pleasantness of evening time and the cool, sweet rain."

That's what their love had been in younger days. It was young and precious beyond words, so full of hope. Then the plant began to fade and gradually become hard and less fragrant. Its buds quit forming. Finally, it is as if some giant harvester hand took the fruit of the wheat, leaving only the brown stalks and stubble. Everything left was devoid of feeling, dead and useless.

Maybe that was it. Perhaps the time of harvest in their life had come and gone. They had obviously lost their chance to love each other fully, and what they had once felt for each other had died—had gradually died, just as her mother had eventually passed away. Maybe Anna knew all this and had been very wise in ending it now. She obviously felt that way.

"I love you, Tom. I just can't marry you. It's too late! Goodbye, Tom!"

Too late.

Goodbye.

A mirage of water lay in the road ahead of Tom as his car sped along. The prairie illusion was always there on the flat roads of the Oklahoma Panhandle, glimmering and beckoning, but it always moved along ahead of him so that he never quite caught up with it.

Anna's love had been a mirage.

Too late.

"I just can't marry you."

He beat his fist on the steering wheel. Eventually his

anger and frustration dissipated. Suddenly the mirage reminded him more and more of Higa. He wondered if her love was fleeting, too, or would her love for him still be alive, fragrant and yielding, as it was when he left her.

It must be, for she had claimed to be immortal, to be eternally youthful. She would still be as beautiful as the day he left her. She would still have the same sparkling black eyes and the full red lips that tugged down at the corners when she smiled. And she would still be waiting. She had promised.

Anna had made her decision—"It's too late!" So he would make his decision, too.

Higa was calling to him now from the glimmering mirage in the road ahead and from the August heat waves that shimmered upward at the edge of the sky, from the plumes of dust and chaff that spiraled up from the plows and from the wind that whipped at his elbow, calling low and enticingly, a voice with a promise, tugging, demanding, "Come back, come back. Love is young—love is immortal!"

Waves be still
And quiet wind;
The Deep and Endless
Waits to speak!

8

The late afternoon sun shone brightly over the ranch buildings, but the new metal granaries, still under construction, reflected the sun with a blinding brilliance in Tom's eyes as he stood in front of the garage. The house was silent.

His eyes caught the shining turn of the windmill's wheel, and he watched its idle movements, smiling as it emitted its old familiar and comforting groans with each slow thrust of its sucker rod into the earth. Tom stretched and breathed deeply. It felt sweet and warm to his lungs.

He heard the clanking sound of metal against metal. He took a few steps in the direction where he heard the sound. In the past few days, with Mrs. Taylor's funeral, he had hardly noticed the progress on the new granaries.

As he strained to hear, Benjamin's voice came to him like the muted battle cry of a general above the scraping metallic clanks and the scrambling noises of his hired men. Tom walked quickly closer to the construction site.

"Get the bolts snugged up tight now. I don't want these bins busting apart and spilling wheat onto the ground this winter. Dammit, Willie, get those men going over there. It'll soon be sundown."

It was his father, all right. He was overseeing the small crew that had remained after harvest to help put together the new granaries to hold the 40-bushel an acre bumper crop. Tom could see his father clearly now. He was standing on a truck bed, pacing back and forth, waving his arms and shouting. His voice was hard as the metal of the grain bins.

"Hello, son," Benjamin said, briefly taking his eyes away from the working men. "So, how were the preacher and his daughter?"

"Fine." Apparently he knew everything that had happened. Why not? His father always seemed to know everything about anything. Some things never changed.

"I was sorry to hear about his missus dying," his father spoke evenly. "It's a helluva note. Nothin's worse. I should know."

"They seem to be taking it okay."

That was it. There was no more discussion of the Taylor family, nor was there any mention of removal from the will for spending time with Anna. Death had caused a truce, however temporary.

"We're in the middle of a hellish hot job here," Benjamin said matter-of-factly. "You know we had to pile thousands of bushels of wheat on the ground when we ran out of space, and I'm not selling it yet to the damned thieves at the grain elevator in Guymon or Hough or Liberal until they go up on the price."

Tom listened without talking.

"Willie and his crew—what's left of 'em—could damn sure use another hand out here," the rancher said. It was more of a challenge than a request. "You better get those fancy pants off, put on some work clothes and get the hell on out here with us."

"All right, Dad," Tom said.

Tom walked back toward the house. He heard his father say something to Willie, and everyone laughed. He tried not to imagine what was said. Even if it were about him, it wouldn't matter much longer. Soon he would be out of the way.

Harriett was standing in front of the kitchen range stirring the contents of several large, steaming kettles. She jumped, turning quickly when Tom walked into the room. She seemed frightened until she realized who he was. She pushed her steamy glasses up on her forehead and peered questioningly at him. Then a broad smile quickly appeared on her face and her color returned.

"Oh! Tom Bristow. You scared me half to death." She sat down heavily by the kitchen table and pushed a chair toward Tom. "I'm sorry about Mrs. Taylor. I know it's hit you hard. But I'm so glad to see you back here today." Her eyes reddened and she dabbed at them with a corner of her apron.

"What's the matter?"

"I worried about your daddy. I think Willie's up to no good. Your dad is so busy driving himself and the men that he doesn't see what's going on around him. I've tried to tell him, but you know what it's like—he won't listen."

"Harriett, what do you mean about Willie?"

She was very upset. That was clear. She had always been so quiet and calm before.

Harriett got up out of her chair and looked nervously out the kitchen door and window and then, in low whispering tones, said, "Willie Lusby has come around here a few times when your Dad isn't here. He's been asking questions. He's got a lot of the devil in him, and I think he's planning something against Mr. Bristow. I just don't know what it is." She dabbed at her eyes with her apron again as Tom realized for the first time that she was uniquely attached to his father, that somehow she had formed a loyalty to him, a protecting fondness like that of a loyal mama bulldog. He wondered if his father appreciated it or if he even knew it existed.

"And the other day I caught him outside Mr. Bristow's office window, peeking in at your father."

Tom patted her shoulder unable to think of anything to say. Finally she raised her head and wiped her eyes on her apron. "I tried to talk to your father about it this morning but..."

"Don't worry anymore about it, Harriett. I'll talk to him," Tom spoke loudly so she could hear. Tom left her, changed quickly and stopped by the kitchen to see Harriett as he made his way out of the house.

"Willie, I'd put Tom to work bolting those sections together over there with Henry," Benjamin said as soon as Tom arrived back at site of the new granaries. "Give him some wrenches and get him at it. The day's nearly over."

Willie Lusby was up on the truck platform with Benjamin. The large crew chief leaned against the cab of the truck, a cigarette dangling nonchalantly from his mouth. He moved quickly when Benjamin spoke, picking up a wrench from the open tool box near his feet and then leaning over to hand it to Tom. He almost swaggered back to his reclining position by the truck's cab, taking no pains to conceal a gloating grin.

Since Tom first started working with the crew, Willie had relished the fact that he, not Benjamin's son, was in charge. Tom could feel his leering eyes on his back as he began tightening the bolts that Henry had put in place.

Tom tried to think through what Harriett had told him. On the one hand, Willie must be doing a satisfactory job or Benjamin wouldn't have kept him around. Benjamin had hired and fired more men than most farmers or ranchers would ever meet, so he was obviously a pretty good judge of character:

Tom was on his fourth bolt when it happened. The wrench he was tugging came flying off of the nut he was tightening and his hand scraped sickeningly against the sharp edge of a strip of the granary metal. Blood spurted out like a fountain, spraying a fiery, abstract design against the side of the shiny granary.

"My God, boy, you've got a nasty gash there," a worker named Henry said, his eyes wide with anxiety. "Let me wrap it for you." Tom had seen Henry before, but only at a distance. He was shocked to see that one of his ears was missing. Henry stared at the cut for a moment and then pulled a surprisingly clean handkerchief from his pocket. Tom grabbed a nearby canteen, poured clean water over the gash, then deftly tied the makeshift bandage around the still-flowing wound.

Henry reached in his back pocket and pulled out a pair of rawhide gloves which he offered to Tom. Tom pulled them on quickly, thanking the one-eared man for his kindness.

All of the men had stopped their work at the sight of the blood spurting against the bright metal. They stayed where they were, gaping as the hand was bandaged. Tom glanced up at the truck once and saw Benjamin and Willie both straining to see his hand. Benjamin said nothing and there was no evidence of sympathy in his face. Willie's grin diminished for a moment, then Tom heard him shout, "Alright men, let's get on with the work. Let's not let a little nick stop the whole show."

"You can go to the house and clean it up if you want," Tom heard his Dad saying.

"I'm okay!" Tom shot back. He wasn't. The gash hurt like hell, but something about the situation kept him going. He wasn't going to wimp out in front of Willie and the other workers, much less in front of his father.

The clanking of the wrenches resumed immediately.

Tom looked up at his father and Willie again. Benjamin looked quickly away from him and commenced talking to Willie in low, inaudible tone.

Pain zigzagged like electricity through Tom's hand and up his arm. He felt nausea cramping at his insides from the loss of blood, but he picked up his wrench and resumed tightening the same nut he had been working on before. As if to erase what had happened, he wiped the drying blood off the razor-sharp metal edge with his shirt sleeve.

Tom worked the rest of that evening, then all of the next day and the next, lifting and tugging at the metal granary sections, slippery and sharp, straining at his wrench, more cautious now of the treacherously sharp corners. He kept his cut hand bandaged carefully and encased safely inside the rawhide glove. The hand throbbed with pain for a couple of days with each jarring turn of his wrench, but he refused to let it be known, not even to Henry who asked him about it occasionally.

His father didn't ask about the hand. With the medical degree pursuit over, what was the point of worrying about the injury?

In a way, Tom was thankful for the pain in his hand: It kept him from thinking about Anna and their lost love. It kept him from focusing on Benjamin and Willie as they strutted about on the truck's platform looking down at the working men, sometimes blasting out curt instructions and sometimes just looking at them, saying nothing. Benjamin especially became more unbearable as the pressure of getting the granaries finished increased. The unprotected wheat piles would be ruined by rain, and multiplied thousands of dollars of crop would be lost.

The days blurred together in a continuous circle of sore muscles, resentment, skinned knuckles, contempt, sweaty bodies bending together under the stove-hot strips of metal. Tom lost track of the days of the week until he saw the dateline on Benjamin's newspaper one morning as he sat with him at the breakfast table.

"We'll finish the rest of the granaries today and tomorrow we'll start scooping wheat into them," Benjamin said as he flipped the paper to one side and began buttering a piece of toast.

"What about Willie?" Tom asked as casually as possible. "How long is he staying around here?"

"What's it to you?" The starkness of his father's question seemed to peel away any hope of civility.

"There's something about him I don't like."

"Well, I'll say it again," Benjamin gruffly responded, "what's it to you?"

"He's..." Tom knew his words were falling on deaf ears.

"He's what?" The rancher challenged. "He's a little rough? He's a bully with the other men? He's crude. Does that bother you?"

"Forget it!"

"No, I won't forget it!" Benjamin poised his egg-laden fork in mid-air—"I want to know what your problem is."

"Harriett told me..."

"Yeah, I know what the old bird thinks about Willie. She told me the other day. You think I don't know Willie would rob me blind or lie to his own mother if he had the chance? So what?"

"Like I said," Tom breathed deeply, "forget it."

"I don't think so," his dad replied evenly. "I think it's good that you've seen for a few days what I've had to put up with running this ranch and farm all these years. I've had every renegade, cut-throat and thief coming here wanting work or a hand-out. Some of them end up making good hired hands and some of them I have to run off. I've been threatened, had knives pulled on me and even been shot at a couple of times. And you know why I put up with the likes of lunkhead oafs like Willie?"

"Why?"

"So I could provide the best life I could for you and your Mama."

"And I appreciate all you've done…"

"No you don't!" His father cut him off. "I've worked all my life to give you the chance I didn't get because I had to quit college during the damned Depression and take care of my own Mama and little brothers and sisters when my own dad ran off to California with some nice Christian woman from Hugoton, and we never heard from him again."

"I didn't make him take off, Dad! And I don't know why you're jumping on me about this now."

"There's a lot you don't know," his father shot back. "I've done my damnedest to provide a way for you to never have to put up with farm machinery or rip your hands up or deal with the likes of Willie. And you blew it all away for that preacher's daughter."

"Quitting school had nothing to do with her," Tom lied.

"This is your Dad you're talking to." Benjamin replied coolly. "She was a big part of your decision to quit school, and I'll never forgive her or her preacher daddy for that. Never!"

"What?"

"And you know what I've already told you about her. Her mama's funeral is over. You've paid your respects. What's done is done. Now, leave her alone."

"Why are you saying…"

Benjamin continued his tirade—"…and if I ever catch you with that girl again, you and I are through, Tom. You'll never get a foot of the Hawk Ranch, even when I'm dead and gone."

Tom drained the last of his coffee, got up from the table and walked back over to the kitchen window, straining to keep his temper in check. He looked out at the calm morning, starkly contrasted to the storm brewing inside the house. The gaunt windmill, the waiting trucks, the slumbering bunkhouse, the dew-hazed green of the golf course—all stood motionless.

"Dad," he exhaled the breath he had been holding tensely, "I do want Anna Taylor, but she doesn't want me. You think she's not good enough for me. Truth is, I'm not good enough for her."

Tom could see Benjamin flinch at that; his pride was laid bare to his soul as he heard the comparison to the despised preacher and his daughter.

"That's a switch," Benjamin shouted, struggling to maintain control as he rose to his feet. "By God, you're lucky to get out of it that cheap. If you know what's good for you, you'll forget her."

"No, I'll never forget her," Tom said, turning to face his father. "She's too good for me and I can never have her, but I'll never forget her."

He studied the livid face of his father a moment, then he added, "And if you want me to leave right now, I will leave the Hawk Ranch for good. It's up to you. All I know is that you aren't telling me what to do with my life any more. And you're not going to tell me who I can be with. Do you understand?"

Perhaps for the first time ever, Tom's soul was laid bare, naked, before his father. He had actually stood up to Benjamin, right or wrong. Let the chips fall where they may. An ocean of bittersweet feelings rushed into the vacuum created by the moment. One of the feelings was sheer exultance, as if he was coming out of a long tunnel into the sun light.

He could see Benjamin more clearly now. He was stripped of his outer shell of puissance and austerity. For a moment Tom shuddered at what he saw. He pitied the hard, twisted man—his father—who had failed himself to be what he desired most in life, and who was now seeing the hard-fought, ever-controlling dreams for his own son dissolving before his eyes.

The chasm between them was fixed. It was too wide for communication. Outside of a dangling footbridge where they had once stood together and shared a sort of filial love, there was now no evidence that they had ever possessed anything in common except the woman—the older man's wife and the younger man's mother—whom they shared.

There were no formalities. Benjamin muttered something about the sun already being up and needing to get the day started. Stopping only long enough to get his hat from behind the kitchen door, he looked fiercely at his only son, shook his head wordlessly, then walked quickly out the door toward the bunkhouse.

Harriett had been busy among her clanking pots and had pretended to hear nothing of the breakfast row. She looked up from her work, almost startled, when Tom came from his bedroom a little later carrying two suitcases. He had packed them with everything he owned that he ever hoped to see again.

"You aren't leaving for good are you?" Harriett asked. "You can't leave now with that Willie Lusby sneaking around here behind Mr. Bristow's back." Her lips trembled as she spoke.

"He'll be alright. My Dad's too tough to get hurt. He can take care of himself. And he has made it clear that he's pretty much given up hope on me. I think it's time for me to leave."

"Where will you go?"

"I don't know."

He did know, but he wasn't going to tell her that he was taking the money he had made from working on the harvesting crew, along with the leftover bank account funds, and he was going to buy a plane ticket for a trip to the other side of the globe.

Harriett stood watching him, her shoulders drawn up

tight, a tenseness in her eyes and mouth that seemed to prevent her from speaking.

Tom pushed open the screen door with one of his suit cases and walked out. Halfway to the garage he turned to see Harriett standing in the doorway, tense and frigid, as though captive of this strange fear that possessed her. Poor, simple, beset, burden-bedeviled woman—she would never know the freedom he was already feeling.

As Tom was getting in his car, he could hear the clanging of the men's wrenches against the metal of the new bins. But above it all he could hear the echoing sharpness of one man's voice, his father's.

Tom started to back his shiny maroon convertible out of the garage. He stopped and gazed over the buildings of the Hawk Ranch. The new, almost-finished granaries stood like giant silver trophies, shining brilliantly in the sun. But they were Benjamin's trophies, his alone.

9

As he sat in his idling automobile, surveying the ranch, he noticed a big black Cadillac coming up the driveway. Waiting a moment to see who it was, he finally spied the passengers—Judge Anson and his daughter Jeanie.

"Where you going, Tom?" the judge asked as he pulled alongside the convertible.

"Just a few errands," Tom lied. "But they can wait. Let me drive my car back into the garage, and I'll help you with your suitcases."

Only then did he remember that his father had mentioned the planned visit. His mind raced. The Ansons would only be at the Hawk Ranch for a few days. He could postpone his departure. It would be fun to have the laughter and jauntiness the judge seemed to take with him everywhere he went. Jeanie was becoming quite a looker, too. It would be fun to have someone else close to his age to listen to music, swim and play golf. Okinawa and Higa could wait.

"Why not?" he asked himself. "I can leave when they leave. Maybe the old man and I can keep a truce for a few days."

"We have visitors," Benjamin said as he came over to welcome his old friend. His dad even smiled at Tom as he spoke, but Tom knew the display of cheeriness was merely to make his guests feel at ease.

"Yep, Jeanie's been bored sick this summer, home from Austin and all. I guess Amarillo is pretty tame compared to the big ole university life. So she's been after me to take her someplace, and that's why I called you," Judge Anson explained. "Here we are, lock, stock and golf clubs. Jeanie thinks she's a golfer, now that she's playing those pretty green courses around UT." He gave her a fatherly tap on the shoulder and guffawed loudly.

Jeanie's tanned face grimaced in faked pain and her long lashes flashed toward Tom as though to see if he was still watching her. Tom looked away quickly toward her father, moving forward to shake hands with him. There was an aura of excitement about the judge and his daughter that never failed to catch Tom's fancy. Jeanie had grown no taller, but her formerly skinny frame had filled out to delightful proportions.

"Hello, Tom," she said smiling. Then she teased, "Do you always greet your guests without a shirt?"

Tom felt his face reddening. Only then did he realize that he had taken off his shirt for the convertible ride. His bare arms and shoulders were tanned and broadened from working on the farm that summer.

He excused himself and walked hurriedly to his bedroom, remembering at that moment that all his good clothes were in a suitcase in the trunk of his car. He heard the judge say loudly for all to hear, "If I had shoulders like that, Tom, I wouldn't wear a shirt, either." The laughter resounded down the hallway as he took the side door out to the garage and the maroon Ford, grabbed his suitcases, then headed back into the house. No one noticed as he went into his room and closed the door. He smiled as he studied his bronzed shoulders in the mirror, then he heard Benjamin laughing at something the judge said. Maybe Judge Anson would melt Benjamin's iciness, he thought. These next few days might be what everybody needs around here.

Harriett had prepared well for the guests. By evening, after a round of golf, she served an incredible meal of barbequed brisket and roasted corn-on-the-cob. Afterward, Benjamin mixed drinks, and he and the judge began recalling favorite memories. It truly seemed like old times, even between the rancher and son.

At one point during the evening, Benjamin even put his hand on Tom's shoulder. The contact was brief, and Tom knew it was well-placed for the benefit of the judge and Jeanie, yet it filled Tom's eyes with a flurry of hot tears for an instant. The warmth, though dramatized, was like it used to be when Tom would come home from school during vacation periods. He fought back an urge to say something affectionate to his father, knowing it would seem out of place in front of their visitors.

As the evening progressed, Tom and Jeanie exchanged polite comments about her plans for the fall school term at the University of Texas. Both avoided any mention of Tom's plans, or lack of plans. Apparently Benjamin had filled in the judge on what had transpired, and Judge Anson had likely passed along the information to Jeanie.

No problem. There was little room for the younger couple's conversation anyway, since most of the attention was focused on the two older men as they reminisced.

Tom's thoughts wandered away to Anna, yet those thoughts were quickly pushed away as he chanced quick glances at Jeanie's enticing blue eyes or a rustling of her petticoats and dark purple skirt as she shifted her shapely, well-tanned legs on the couch beside him.

Later that evening, Tom stood in his pajamas in his bedroom, near the door that led to the hallway, musing on what Jeanie was doing at that same moment. She had retired to one of the guest rooms across the hall just a few moments before, and he could hear her moving around in her room. He could still smell her perfume. Lying back on his bed, he let himself imagine lustfully what Jeanie was wearing or not wearing at that precise moment. In his mind, she was standing in front of the full-length mirror brushing her hair, in a flimsy silk gown that enhanced the shapeliness of her enticing, tender body.

The Bristow and Anson foursome were on the number one tee by nine the following morning. By lunch-time they had played eighteen holes of golf. Tom and Jeanie laughed like children at her puffing father as he plowed about the fairways. The judge followed his frequent quips with his deep, roaring laughter that could probably be heard all the way to Goff Creek. Jeanie looked often at Tom out of the corners of her eyes and smiled, then they would both break into laughter of their own that would end as quickly as it started. Jeanie's laughing was like tinkling bells in the wind.

"Father, you're just like a boy with a new choo-choo toy," Jeanie chided him after a particularly good drive, referring to his new Ben Hogan signature golf clubs. If he happened to hit the ball extra well, she would run up to him and dance a jig about him and cheer him on. The carefully tailored shorts she wore emphasized and revealed even more of her alluring shapeliness than last night. He tried not to stare at her long tanned legs. A red and white striped shirt, disarmingly snug, spoke volumes to him with every bounce of her lithe body. She skipped along with her honey-silken hair blowing out behind her and her blue eyes dancing to the beat of her feet.

Tom found himself comparing her with Anna. Jeanie seemed so much younger. She was pretty, in a delightful way, because she seemed to have absolutely no cares in the world. She obviously knew how to live and to enjoy herself. That was very attractive to Tom—now, more than ever.

The next morning Tom awoke to a soft baying sound outside his door. At first it remarkably resembled a coyote howling at a distance, but after raising his head from his pillow and listening more acutely, he realized the sound was coming from the hall just outside his bedroom door. He crept quietly to the door and as he anticipated, found Jeanie crouched outside his door imitating a coyote, both with her wails and posture. She was wearing a bathing suit that matched the languid blueness of her eyes. The elastic fabric held snugly to her rounded hips, left the straight, tanned back bare and the cups in front clinging miraculously to her rounded feminine curves. She stood up on her knees, pawing at his legs with her hands in her continued effort to play the part of a coyote. From his height, standing above her, her breasts almost seemed to swell up free of the swim suit, tantalizingly close. He watched her, saying nothing, frozen in his pleasure.

She hopped to her feet and said, "Too much sleep makes Tom a dull boy. Let's take a dip."

Tom was fascinated at the vigor tugging within her swim suit, and he continued to stare at her for more than a polite moment before managing to stammer something about meeting her at the pool. He was into his suit in seconds and caught up with her in the kitchen where she had stopped to get a drink of water. As Tom started out the door, Jeanie ran up beside him and said enthusiastically, "I'll race you to the pool!"

It was not a large pool, certainly not as large as the public pools in Guymon or Amarillo, but it fit perfectly with the Hawk Ranch house. Benjamin had it built the past spring just a few feet from the house, apparently as a surprise for Tom's anticipated return to intern and practice medicine in Guymon.

Tom's long legs easily outdistanced Jeanie, so he reached the edge of the pool first. When he turned to wait for her, she darted past him. Without missing a stride, she dove in and swam the full length of the pool underwater. She came up splashing and spewing, then after a moment of clearing the water from her eyes and seeing Tom hadn't yet entered the water, she swam over to him. He reached his hand down to her. She took it and he pulled her up beside him.

The excitement as their bodies touched was like a strong current of electricity that jetted through his veins. He felt a sudden desire to capture this wild creature and hold her close, tamed, tanned and motionless against him. She looked at him playfully for a moment and then pirouetted and dove back into the water.

The visit of Judge Anson and his daughter consumed the next two days. Tom realized that he had hardly thought of Anna at all. He thought about calling her, but golfing and swimming all day, then playing bridge in the evenings, left little time for even a phone call. Tom had to admit that he was happy just having a good time. Anyway, Anna had already decided their fate—"I love you, Tom. I just can't marry you. It's too late! Goodbye, Tom!"

Too late? Then it was simply too late. Fine and dandy. Ever onward and upward. Life was too short to dwell on the could-have-beens. Anna was past-tense. It was her choice.

At bridge, as in golf, Tom and Jeanie were always partners and usually had high score. One evening they made two slams in succession which caused the judge to comment in Benjamin's direction, "These kids of ours seem to have a knack of knowing what the other one is thinking. Maybe we should change partners."

"No!" Jeanie said loudly. "He's mine, daddy. Keep your big claws off!" She sounded so possessive, Tom expected to see some sign of embarrassment follow, but she went on playing and talking as cool as the tall glass of Long Island iced tea she was sipping.

The last day of the visit passed rapidly as had the others. They had topped it off with an early dinner on the patio and Harriett was at her best. Her serving manner was not the most polished, but her food was delicious. Even his "meat-and-potatoes" father seemed to relish her succulent Greek moussaka, baked with its layers of ground lamb, sliced aubergine and tomato, topped with a tasty white sauce. A dry red wine, imported from Domaine Harlaftis in the Attika region of Greece was the perfect addition to the meal, and Tom joined the three others at the table, warmed by the dark garnet liquid.

A rare combination of slight summer breezes and no insects prevailed, enabling them to enjoy their food on the terrazzo-tiled patio to the utmost. Everyone had been unusually quiet during the meal and Tom attributed it to their thoughts that this would be their last evening together—that their interlude of golf and bridge would soon be ended. His thoughts were confirmed by the special warm manner employed in their treatment of each other—that special warmth that comes when separation is imminent.

The judge apparently could tolerate the silence no longer. During dessert—one of Harriett's more exotic concoctions, an assortment of fresh peaches, apricots, apples and cantaloupe mixed with whipped cream between layers of crispy pastry—he showered his listeners with an avalanche of legal issues involving a boundary dispute that had arose during a recent expansion of the Hawk Ranch properties. He and Benjamin decided they would forego bridge for the evening to go through papers concerning the boundary matters.

"Boundaries-schmounderies, such dull goings on," Jeanie said mockingly as the two fathers headed for Benjamin's paneled office. She flounced from the table to a glider and stretched her bare legs into a reclining position that, despite her flippancy, Tom thought was graceful enough to capture the eye of any artist.

The sun was hidden behind the western horizon, yet a few remnants of rose-hued light still splotched the beige stone of the house, the glider and Jeanie's beautifully tapered legs. Tom stared at her uncontrollably. She looked up at him out of the corners of her eyes, her long lashes at half-mast, as though she liked his staring, but that it was not nearly enough.

With sudden boldness, Tom bent down and pulled her up into a sitting position and sat down close beside her. She put her arms about his neck as though to keep herself from falling. From the way she clung to him, he knew she hadn't objected to his move. The way she kept looking at him seemed obvious that she wanted more than his stares, much more.

"Let's go for a ride in my convertible," he said. "I'll take down the top."

"Beg me," she said with a teasing toss of her blond head.

Tom relaxed against the back of the glider. "The moon is eloquent and riding high," he said, going along with her teases. "The night is tailor-made for a ride in yon chariot." He voiced the last few words in low, enticing tones, mocking the boudoir intonations he had heard in movies.

"I'd rather go for a walk," Jeanie said, jumping suddenly to her feet as though the matter were settled. The action was so unexpected it almost threw Tom from the glider. He caught his balance and stood up.

"You might get a little chilly in those shorts and thin top," he said, harassingly.

"I'm used to it," she said, jumping up and down beside him like a little girl. "Besides, you can keep me nice and warm. Let's go."

They walked a little apart, Tom with long, measured strides and Jeanie with little skips. Occasionally she would bump against his arm, just slightly, but each time it sent a current of energized magic flitting through his body.

The moon appeared to be a great orange balloon rising on a string to greet them. Its light cast an effulgent glow over the ranch buildings and enhanced the gloss of the golden wheat stubble. It glimmered against the windmill so intensely that long, black shadows stretched almost all the way from its base to the swimming pool. The windmill had stopped its liquid groanings for the evening, as if in awe of the stillness that lay all about them. It was like being part of a beautiful painting that had suddenly come to life, moving about on a gigantic canvas. The vista they shared pulled them closer together, and they walked now arm in arm, more slowly than at first. Tom could feel the eager energy within her, bridled now, but prancing to be loosed.

They strolled silently along a path that led through one of the stubble fields and around the ranch buildings to the golf course. Tom thought the way the golf course sprawled out its green fairway fingers into the wheat stubble, it seemed so out of place in the empty, straw-covered flatness and the overlay of stars that were eons apart, yet so very near.

"Do you like this golf course?" Tom asked, feeling that the sound of his voice had almost been lost in this large stillness around them.

"Yes, I think it's fun. I think every ranch out here in the Oklahoma Panhandle should have one." Jeanie laughed at her own joke and looked up at Tom with a sly knowingness from the corners of her eyes.

"I mean—don't you think it's a little out of place

here—here where there is nothing to go with it except wheat and wind and space and..." Tom arced his hand across the sky, "and all that—all that—whatever it is that's up there. Where did all those planets come from? Why should we be a part of all this and still not know all the answers?"

"What do we care about that, you big galoot," She said. "We will never know. Why worry about the big questions? It's all just to look at. We are here and the things up in the heavens are beautiful and that's all that matters. It's up to us down here to enjoy all of that beauty...and each other." She stood so close that he could feel the warmth of her bare legs through his slacks.

They had stopped on the number five fairway near the green. Tom laughed at Jeanie's complete lack of understanding of what he had been saying. There was a bewitchment about her that made her effervescent spirit even more exciting. Yet there was a tenderness within her that saved her from appearing too forward. He pulled her tightly against his body and felt no resistance. To the contrary, she seemed to expect his kisses, to desire them, and her response was so eager and spontaneous he quickly forgot the matter of the displaced golf course and whether it did or didn't fit in with its surroundings of wheat, wind and space.

Her lips were a warm mixture of honey and liquid sunshine, and the taste set off that same exciting current of energy he had felt at the pool that morning. It surged through him again and again, and he could feel himself being drawn closer and closer to her compelling warmth, to this force within her that was love and at the same time consumed love. He could feel the firmness of her breasts against him, and with each yielding movement of her body, he knew she was his—that he had captivated her, that she was captivating him. This fleshly love that grasped at him and sought to devour him, surely it was the answer to all he had ever hoped for. It was more than physical love. He had tasted that before. This was freedom and wild abandonment. She was incredibly warm and willing. Together they felt the magnetism grow into a white-hot heat that could not be contained, and it swept over the two young bodies like an all-consuming prairie wildfire.

He dared not think of Anna, nor of Higa, nor of anything nor anyone in the world except Jeanie—for the moment. He focused all of his energy, all his senses, upon her pleasure. There was nothing in his mind but Jeanie and her warm, eager responsiveness. She was here with him now. She was all he wanted. Her breaths tantalized him, enflamed him, and together they fueled each other to irrepressible, sweeping heights of passion.

10

Tom and Jeannie spoke few words during the passionate scene on the fifth fairway. Afterward, as they walked back to the ranch house, she held his hand. As they walked silently through the hallway, she gave him a tender goodnight kiss and headed for her room. He thought about asking her to spend the night with him, but decided it would make everyone feel awkward if either Benjamin or the judge discovered them together.

The next morning, he went to her room and sat on the side of her bed.

"About last night," he began. "I want you to know…"

"You were great" she laughed spontaneously. "I was great. It was great. That's enough for me."

"That's it?" he quizzed her.

"What do you want?" she smiled warmly, "a marriage proposal?" She laughed. "Honestly, Tom, it's okay. I don't need anything except maybe an encore performance the next time we're together. I'm not the clinging vine type."

"But you and I…"

"We had fun," she reached out to touch his hand. More electricity! "That's all I wanted from you. That's all I want out of life. Anything else doesn't do it for me!"

"But what about you and me?"

"Ohmigosh!" Jeanie exclaimed softly. "Ohmigosh, Tommy. You thought...?"

"Jeanie, I could truly fall in love with you," Tom said, moving closer beside her on the bed. "I've never been with anyone like you. We've known each other for years. And you know how happy the Judge and my Dad would be if we ever got together. They would love it."

"Ohmigosh!" she said again. "I really like you, but I just don't love you. I don't know if I'll ever love anyone enough to settle down. Certainly not any time soon. I've gotta have excitement. I wanna have fun while I'm young. Nobody's gonna tie me down, not even someone as luscious and wonderful as you, Tom Bristow."

He didn't know what to say.

"Oh, posh," she continued. "Don't look so glum. We'll get back together soon and have another good time together. And who knows, maybe we'll do it on the fifth fairway during the daytime. Wouldn't that be a lark?"

Judge Anson's black Cadillac took her away that morning. He could see her leaning back complacently in her seat, looking at him from the corners of her eyes with an expression of mischievous secrecy at what had passed between them. She smiled mischievously one last time and waved as the car headed out the driveway. Tom waved back, lost in thought as he watched the luxury automobile pass out of view, headed back to Amarillo.

Jeanie had been a whirlwind that had rushed over him suddenly, stirred him into frenzy and then passed on, leaving him feeling desolate, empty and windswept.

In less than a week, he had gone down in flames at the hands of two very different women.

Pure, sweet Anna, guided by some illogical path, said, "I love you, Tom. I just can't marry you. It's too late!

Goodbye, Tom!"

The end.

Magical, mischievous, whimsical, fun-loving Jeanie had said, "I really like you. I just don't love you."

Another bitter ending.

Neither cruel conclusion made sense to him, but it was just as well. It was too late for Anna; that door was slammed shut. And Jeanie was gone, riding her own personal whirlwind.

His father left soon after the Anson's departure, headed for Oklahoma City to meet with two senators about the "thieves running the grain business." Tom was not invited nor included, nor did he want to be. He was glad to be alone with his thoughts of Anna, then Jeanie, and finally of Higa.

Higa.

Always and immortal.

Exotic Higa.

Tom knew what he wanted to do. He carefully took the beautiful magatama out of the box in his waiting suitcase and fingered it tenderly, gazing at the greenish gem, thinking of his lost love waiting halfway around the globe.

If he had learned anything during the past few days, it was more apparent now than ever that he knew absolutely nothing about women. Perhaps it was time to travel to the one woman who seemed to know the most important secret of all. After all she wanted to give that priceless secret of immortality to him.

11

The Pacific at 12,000 feet looked like a wash board splotched with patches of gray and ivory suds. Tom wished he could trade the monotonous humming of the plane's motors for the swishing, rolling rumbles of the white caps. He had tried to sleep like the other passengers but the excitement of knowing he would soon be in Okinawa with Higa had precluded sleep, except for sporadic snatches. He didn't feel like he belonged here in this consortium of snoring, sagging soldiers and sailors with their jaws dropped on their chests, their arms and legs jutting out in humorous positions.

Tom switched on an overhead reading light and spent part of the flight going through a dog-eared National Geographic article about Okinawa and that country's interesting people. As he read, he remembered more and more that Higa had told him about her people. He was also fascinated to learn more about the world's longest-living people who inhabit what once was called the Kingdom of the Ryukyus. The magazine explained that the Okinawans boasted the world's largest number of centenarians and the healthiest elderly population on the planet. Tom was amazed to read that the islands were sometimes called "the Land of the Happy Immortals."

"Maybe there really is something to what Higa told me," Tom's heart beat faster. "Maybe she does know the secret."

For centuries, the Ryukyus had drawn the attention of neighboring countries. In fact, history records that in 219 B.C., the Emperor of China sent 3,000 young men and women with a cargo of seeds to the "islands of the Eastern seas" to find the legendary "happy immortals" purported to dwell there. Ironically, history also records that no one returned from that voyage since apparently the people settled either on Okinawa or other peaceful Japanese islands. Yang Chien of the Chinese Sui dynasty (580-618 A.D) also referred to "the happy immortals," as did the legendary explorer Marco Polo (1254-1324), who learned of the islands south of Japan that reportedly held the secrets to immortality, though he never discovered what or where those secrets were.

Tom looked up from the magazine to see that the day's first hint of sun now illuminated the plane's otherwise drab interior with red hues. Looking down at the sea below him, he could see the rouging effects of the dawning sun on the foaming waters. He watched for a long time through his narrow window as the ocean's face went from grey to red, then gold, then faded gradually into a full, naked and daring blue.

As the morning grew older, soldiers and sailors sat up in varying stages of rumpled disorder, lighting cigarettes and taking turns at their abbreviated toiletries. The smell of bacon and eggs teased their nostrils for a few moments; then they were all in their seats laughing, nodding at one another and gesturing as they talked and ate.

The Happy Immortals

Tom wondered at their gaiety, for all they had to look forward to was a stretch of duty on an island that would be dull and meaningless. None of them knew Higa, and only she had brought life to him during his time on the island. He wished he could tell them all about Higa and her secret to immortality. Maybe Higa would choose him to release her secret to the whole world.

During the years he had carried Higa and her secret about with him, he had never dared to believe that he would actually go back to Okinawa. He had thought his obsession would gradually wear itself out and at times it had almost left him completely, but always the exhilarating sparkle of madness would return.

He felt in his pocket for the magatama. The curved iridescent gem met his fingers warmly, and he smiled as he finished the last of his scrambled eggs. Now he would know the truth after all these years of waiting. He would soon know everything about Higa's secret.

"She will have kept the secret so long she'll be bursting to spill it out," Tom thought, almost shuddering with anticipation.

The morning wore on, and just before noon Tom's ears began popping. Soon a voice over the speakers grated out the news that they were nearing Okinawa and commencing their descent. Tom fastened his seat belt as instructed, along with the other passengers, and peered out the small window to his left. He was sitting in front of the port wing, and as the plane angled its nose downward and banked slightly, he could see almost the full length of Okinawa. It was disappointingly unimpressive; it looked like a huge green worm that had crawled off from the rest of the world to die. In World War II, Tom had approached it from the deck of a ship and at surface level it stood out of the water like a mountain on a plain, and the rich green of its hills had mixed glamorously with the excitement of war. It had left memories that were far more beautiful than what faced him now.

The slow circles of the plane above the island reminded Tom of a hawk gliding in to pounce on a rabbit. The island gradually grew larger with the plane's descent and soon ribbons of asphalt highways appeared, forming an incomplete checker board. Hills rose up from their surroundings and fuzzy patches of greenery in the valleys evolved into trees. Naha and Shuri at the southern end of the island looked drowsy in the midday sun.

The landing was uneventful and so was their reception at Kadena Air Base; no one seemed to care that they had landed. The soldiers and sailors rummaged about lazily for knapsacks and other traveling paraphernalia, stretched their limbs and yawned, obviously bored. It was not at all as Tom had visualized it. His thoughts of returning to Okinawa, though never analyzed in detail, had always included a vision of Higa standing on a high green hill with her arms outstretched, waiting to greet him.

The other passengers brushed past Tom with indifference, and as he walked down the ramp, a hot wind blew dust in his eyes. He thought he had never seen a more desolate and unfriendly place.

Kadena Air Base was a melee of five percent aircraft and ninety-five percent dusty jeeps. The latter darted in all directions with fast starts and faster stops, their stiff-spine drivers pulling at levers and yanking at wheels with the jerky movements of robots. Tom's shirt was soon saturated with perspiration and he was relieved to find a place that was air-conditioned where he could eat his lunch and collect his thoughts. He smiled at the irony of air conditioning on Okinawa. How the troops of his old outfit would have laughed.

After a quick meal, Tom found a limousine that was on its way to Shuri. Calling it a limousine was outlandish. The old Buick sedan was more rust than paint and chrome. Its tires were so worn it appeared they might blow out before going the first mile. The driver was a slim, short Okinawan with teeth so large it seemed they, not his hands, were in control of the car. He smiled continuously and kept taking in more and more riders until there were finally seven passengers besides himself. The grumbling of the passengers appeared not to bother him in the least, judging from his continual, toothy smiles.

All of the passengers were military men except Tom and a heavy jowled man, about 60, who was dressed in a rumpled white suit and a white shirt that clung to each wrinkle of his oversized anatomy. He reminded Tom of Judge Anson, except he didn't talk as much. Tom was curious as to what this well dressed American was doing in Okinawa and made several inquisitive remarks to no avail. He did learn from him, though, of the Rictan House, a small boarding house near the downtown area of Shuri that provided rooms with baths and food much superior to any of the hotels. Tom got the address of the Rictan House, but he never learned anything more of consequence from his heavy, perspiring friend.

When the crickety Buick arrived in Shuri, miraculously, with no blow-outs or break-downs, the heavy man stayed in the limousine, grasping a tightly packed briefcase to his bosom as though it contained his life savings. He merely nodded, sober and appearing almost relieved when Tom and the other passengers got out, leaving him alone with the driver and his shiny teeth.

The Rictan was all the heavy man had told him it would be. The friendly hotel manager spoke English and was helpful in giving Tom directions to find his way about in Shuri. Sadly, the manager had no knowledge of Higa or her family. He wore heavily rimmed glasses and had several missing teeth which were revealed nakedly when he smiled. He smiled often.

"If woman companion you desire, Mr. Bristow, I can

accommodate you well." He winked knowingly behind the eyeglasses. His word "accommodate" was spoken as thought it were a tantalizing menu.

"Oh, no. This girl is something special," Tom hurried to explain, somewhat abashed at the manager's forwardness. He went on to describe her in detail, suddenly aware that Higa looked very similar to thousands of other Okinawan women. This was the beginning of a realization that he might have difficulty finding Higa. It was a crushing thought.

As he stood in the hotel lobby, he heard familiar strains of a song he had heard many times. The singer, decidedly Asian, was butchering the melody, but the words were unmistakably recognizable, even through the thick accent:

You must remember this
A kiss is just a kiss, a sigh is just a sigh.
The fundamental things apply
As time goes by.
And when two lovers woo
They still say, "I love you."
On that you can rely
No matter what the future brings
As time goes by.

He had seen *Casablanca* as a college sophomore for the first time at the old Sooner Theater on East Main Street in Norman, walking distance from his dorm. He remembered watching Humphrey Bogart and Ingrid Bergman in the movie, wondering if he would ever see such an exotic place as occupied Africa during the early days of World War II, if he would be caught up in the war as so many of his friends and classmates were, and if he would someday find his own Ilsa.

Moonlight and love songs

Never out of date.
Hearts full of passion
Jealousy and hate.
Woman needs man
And man must have his mate
That no one can deny.

He stood in the doorway to the lounge, listening to the band and its mediocre singer. The Rican Hotel was certainly no Rick's, and the singer mangling the tune was no Sam, but the song's words came back to him like a long lost friend, reminding him that so much had happened since he first heard Dooley Wilson sing the music for the first time on the big screen. Not only had he seen more war than he wanted to remember, but he had traveled halfway around the globe to Okinawa, found Higa, yet had never totally left Anna behind.

It's still the same old story
A fight for love and glory
A case of do or die.
The world will always welcome lovers
As time goes by.
Oh yes, the world will always welcome lovers
As time goes by.

He turned and moved toward his hotel room, forcing himself to leave the song and its memories behind. He must concentrate on the only one who mattered at the moment.

During all the years he had dreamed of returning to Okinawa, it had never occurred to him that the practical matter of knowing a street address would be of consequence in learning the secret to immortality. The city directories and telephone listings, even with the aid of the Rictan manager, proved fruitless. It seemed as if there were nothing left to do but walk the streets, hoping his intuition would lead him in the right direction.

The busy shops, a curious mix of modern American commercialism and the uniquely ancient oriental, seemed to swarm with people under banner-draped streets. Men walked jauntily along in their panama cone-shaped hats and their long shapeless shirts. Women wore brightly colored kimonos, the more sophisticated ones with gold-threaded obis about their waists. Tom found himself becoming more and more jealous of their happy countenances and apparent contentment with who they were and where they were.

After the fourth day of searching for Higa in Shuri, a drenching rain began falling. Tom remembered that it had rained nearly every day during August when he was there during Word War II. They had dug trenches around their pup tents to drain away the water, and the mess-kits always seemed to fill up with rain before shelter could be found and the food eaten. Now the faces of the Okinawan women all began to look alike in the rain and, each night, Tom would go back to his room, pull off his soggy clothes, sponge the water off his weary body and fall defeated across the bed.

Would he ever see Higa again? Had he already passed her in the crowds, unable to recognize what she looked like with the passing years? The thoughts tormented him.

By the end of the third week of August, Tom decided his intuition was an undependable guide. More out of desperation than design, he rented a car and drove toward the area where his division had bivouacked while it waited for the treaty with Japan to be signed aboard the battle ship Missouri.

Everything seemed so different. If he could just recognize one familiar landmark, he could then perhaps find the burial cave near the place where he used to rendezvous with Higa.

Tom drove slowly along the highway north of Shuri

hoping to find a place he could turn off that would lead him to Higa's burial cave. His enthusiasm grew within him as he drove along and he wondered why he hadn't thought of coming out here in the first place, the logical place to find her, her ancestor's burial cave. It was, after all, the place where he first saw her and where she had come so faithfully back then to pray.

He crossed the Asato River, realizing this couldn't have been the stream where he and Higa had sat under the wooden bridge that day to get out of the rain, since this steam was much too wide. Before he had gone another two miles he spotted a narrow, rutted dirt road leading off among the banyan trees and thickets of bougainvillea. He turned off onto the side road cautiously, for it was still quite muddy from all the recent rains.

Before going two-hundred yards, he heard the rear wheels whining as they spun in the mud. He felt the car lurch sideways a couple of times, so he parked the car, fearful of becoming immobile. He struck off on foot through the damp clumps of grass and the low hanging branches of the banyan trees, which at the slightest touch, would shower him with the water that had accumulated on their leaves.

He walked for several hours, first along a small contributory which he hopefully decided was the one that ran under his and Higa's bridge. Then, after not finding the bridge, he began climbing the hills along the stream. They grew larger and more rolling, like the one that housed Higa's cave. He rushed eagerly, slipping and grasping any deep rooted vegetation available, sometimes half-crawling, to the top of each hill to look longingly ahead to the next hill for any sign of a cave.

Nothing!

He was about to admit defeat and go back to his car, if he could find his car, when on reaching the top of the last hill he had told himself he was going to climb, his heart began racing madly. His breath came out in short spurts as the entrance to a cave appeared. The ruins of Rome could never have looked more beautiful. The stones had been torn away and weeds had grown with ragged abandon about the entrance. There was even a large flat rock nearby like the one he and Higa had used as a dinner table. He was dimly aware of his deplorably muddy trousers as he picked himself up from the downward slope of the hill where he had fallen headlong in his rush to reach the cave.

Higa was not there, nor had anyone been there for years, it appeared, but he relished the thrill of merely seeing Higa's cave again. He dared not allow himself to doubt. He wanted desperately to know that at least that part of his dream with Higa was real, like his magatama. That was enough for the moment.

He slouched exhausted on the rock, studying the desolate condition of the cave's entrance. The silence was consuming and he felt solid, fixed and inanimate, as though he had been here all his days, a part of the still surroundings, as one of the stones that some prying soldier had cast aside in his search for jewels among the urns of death.

Finally, the spell passed and Tom rose from the rock, dragging his weary feet to the cave's entrance. He bent over and crawled through the stony entrance after stopping first to swipe away a network of spider webs. The webs stuck mockingly to his fingers. The damp, cool dirt that formed the packed floor of the cave, felt clammy as he proceeded cautiously inside. The darkness was overwhelming at first, then as his eyes adjusted, the small light from the entrance-way afforded some vision. He saw a small overturned urn, plain, with ugly jagged chips, the end of a human bone protruding as though it were the withered stalk of a long dead potted plant. Looking further into the darkness, he saw other human bones scattered grotesquely like a child's "pick-up-sticks" amid molding ashes. Tom's face suddenly felt flushed and a fit of nausea seized him. The thought of vomiting on the bones and ashes forced him to whirl quickly and plunge in a mad crawling leap through the cave's entrance, back into the blindingly bright sunlight.

He closed his eyes and lay prostrate on the ragged weeds that had been crushed beneath him. Then, as though the sun's bright rays had activated his reasoning, he became acutely aware that this could not have been Higa's cave. There were too many things different about this place. The crushing realization hit him like a sucker punch to his stomach, causing him to exhale in ragged breaths.

It was absolutely, positively NOT the place where he and beautiful Higa had sat so many times and repeated their waka together.

He raised himself up on his elbows and looked around the damp green hills. They seemed to taunt him in their loneliness: "Go away you fool. You don't belong to us. Go back where you came from!"

Years of pent-up emotions seized his heart. His chest convulsed and he heard ugly, hoarse croaks emanating from his throat, as though torn from the very tissue of his heart, partly a primeval form of laughter and mostly the futile sobs of a doomed dream.

"Time is running out," Tom thought, and he dropped his face back against the earth. "Higa is as elusive as her secret of immortality, and I am a fool to be here searching for her. I was a fool to have ever come back to Okinawa. I should have shut her out of my mind years ago. What a cruel hoax I've played on myself."

He shouted out loud to the trees: "I don't believe anything she said about the secret of immortality. It's nothing. I'm nothing. I've failed at everything I've ever done. Now this!"

His words reverberated mockingly among the hills that surrounded him, and he laughed bitterly as he thought of what Benjamin would have said if he could see his son now. And his father would have been absolutely right in his disdain. Tom raised himself up on one elbow and with his free fist, he pounded the earth over and over again, whispering hoarsely, "It's all some cruel joke. I'm such a failure. Everything I've ever believed in is a hoax. What a fool I've been!"

Finally, the blood from his knuckles became indistinguishable from the red mud of the Okinawan hillside where he lay. Again and again, the pounding thuds from his fists smashing the damp earth echoed percussively, savagely through the hillside.

Finally, in complete exhaustion, he dropped his head to the turf, motionless. The warmth of the tears on his face and the warmth of the bright sun coaxed him into a deep slumber.

The still-bright afternoon sun was the first thing of which Tom's sleep-woozy mind became aware when he awoke; then he felt a hand on his wrist. He jumped up with a start. It was not until he had scrambled to his feet that he saw his visitor was a freckle-faced American soldier in fatigues. He stepped back away from Tom, staring at him with quizzical eyes.

"My God, man! You scared the hell out of me for a minute. I thought you was dead—and—and I was just feeling your pulse to see if—if—"

The solider began laughing, mostly from wild relief, then his face wrinkled with an earthy delight.

Tom was embarrassed at being caught asleep out in the country with no apparent reason for being there, but he could think of nothing to say that sounded logical. He was glad his visitor was talkative.

"What the hell are you doing out here all by yourself? Sleeping one off?" He punched Tom on the shoulder playfully with a chubby finger, and laughed, apparently proud of being able to appraise Tom's situation so readily.

"No, I haven't had anything to drink. I've been looking for someone..." Tom's voice trailed off as he pondered the incongruity of his real reason for being there. For a moment, he wished he could tell this soldier, or anyone who would listen, all about Higa and her promise—but, of course, he would laugh and call him a deluded nut.

"I know what's ailing you, fella," the soldier said, putting his hand on Tom's shoulder. "You need a drink. I'm a little thirsty myself and I'm tired of poking around in these caves anyway. Nothing out here in these hills but old bones. All the good stuff's already been lifted." He gave Tom a sly, accusative look. "How do you get off wearing those civvies? What outfit do you belong to anyway?"

"I don't belong to any outfit," Tom said, guardedly. And hoping to allay some of the soldier's inquisitiveness, he said, "I'll take you up on that drink. I've got a car not too far from here."

The car was farther away than he cared to admit, but Tom felt sure it wouldn't matter to this jolly-faced, adventuresome soldier boy. They walked quickly. Tom groaned wordlessly from the soreness of his fists, arms and legs. The soldier talked constantly during the first part of their hike back to the car. He told Tom in detail that his name was Alex; that his full name was Andrew Jamison Alexander, but everyone called him Alex. In fact, he was "damned glad of it because I don't like Andrew or Jamison, either one".

As the tramping up and down the hills wore on, Alex's excess weight forced his huffing and puffing lungs to restrict talk to a minimum.

With less searching than Tom had anticipated, they found the car, but not before the soldier gave him a few doubting glances as to whether he knew where he was going. After a few more dubious moments of wheels spinning heatedly in the muddy ruts, Tom got the car out onto the main road and drove southward toward Naha.

"Just follow this highway right into Naha," freckle-faced Alex said, "and I'll show you a place that's not too crowded, but it's where you can get the best damned drink in the Pacific. It ain't fancy, but you'll like it just fine, I'll guaran-damn-tee."

Tom could not distinguish any name on the front of the crudely tiled front of the tavern where the soldier directed him. Apparently the well-worn place needed no name on the outside to draw passers-by inside. Bells tinkled merrily above their heads as they pushed open the front door. The dim light inside revealed a bar and crude tables that appeared to have once been G.I. footlockers. Two naked light bulbs also outlined several splintered benches beside the footlocker tables.

An Okinawan girl, possibly eighteen, played an eerie melody on a long-necked, fretless, three-stringed apparatus.

"It's a samisen," Alex said, pointing to the lute-looking instrument as the young lady strummed. "You're gonna like this...and her!"

As she deftly strummed the small, square body, the attention of both men was drawn from the catskin covered, curved-back peg box up to the sensuous movements of the woman herself. She slid her bare feet toward Tom and his friend. Her lavender-colored bra and stained bikini with frilly, dangling tassels gave her a well-used, debauched look. She held the samisen tightly across her breasts as she sang with her crooked teeth exposed. Almost indecently, she weaved her way around them as she sang the mournful Japanese melody, the words jerky and grating, her body lithe and captivating. Tom couldn't help but notice that her small rounded eyes stared at no one, yet past everyone, in a lost, terrified look that seemed out of place, even frightening.

The soldier winked at Tom as though to say, "Didn't I tell you—didn't I tell you you'd like this place."

Tom and Alex stood silently for a moment, spellbound by the singing girl. A half dozen soldiers and a couple of native men stood, also transfixed, with their backs to the bar, forgetting their drinks behind them.

Finally, Alex claimed a bench by one of the footlocker tables and motioned Tom to join him. Before Tom could get seated, Alex had ordered sake for both of them. A graying, wrinkled man with a permanently frozen smile brought their drinks with rapidly shuffling feet, bowing briskly a couple of times as he took the money Alex shoved toward him.

A shudder of revulsion went through Tom at the first taste of the dank liquid, and he wondered how Alex could take such voluminous gulps of the stuff. Tom remembered how in Okinawa, sake isn't just an alcoholic beverage made from rice. On this island, it referred to shochu made from sugar cane, or kusu, which was distilled. Either packed a powerful wallop.

Alex didn't seem to care much about the intricacies of the potent drink. He launched into a discourse on comparisons between liquor in his hometown of Wichita and what they had to drink in Okinawa.

As the sake loosened his tongue (as if anything was needed for that!), Alex went from Wichita's liquor to its high school football teams and then to the aircraft facilities where he planned to work when he got his discharge. He spoke with such an exuberance and friendliness that Tom found his conversation preferable to the dreary songs of the samisen strummer.

"After eighteen months of this place it's sure going to be great to get back to those Kansas women." Alex licked his lips, smiling, and he gave Tom a quick, anticipatory look from the corners of his eyes. "They've got it all over these naisons around here." He sighed longingly. "They just don't grow 'em here like they do in Wichita. But, I guess you've found that out for yourself."

"No, I don't know much about the women here," Tom said, wondering what a naison was and at the same time trying not to appear too naïve. "What do you figure is the main difference between our women back home and the ones here?" Tom leaned forward, hoping vaguely that Alex might drop some clue that would help him, at least indirectly, to locate Higa.

"Some of the young ones are okay, but they get old gawd-awful fast here. At thirty, they look like grandmas. Of course the younger ones are pretty lively sometimes." Then he added, as though he weren't sure he had fully impressed Tom, "They'll give you what you want usually, but you want to watch 'em or they'll roll you while they're at it, and you don't have to go down to the Neusegua for that either."

Alex threw down his last swallow of sake and seemed delighted that Tom's puzzlement over the word Neusegua gave him an opportunity to explain that it was an area where prostitutes met incoming military personnel near Naha Harbour and offered their tacitly illicit, pleasurably brief and generally inexpensive services.

Tom decided that Alex had a distorted impression of Okinawan women in general, because the ones he had seen weren't out to roll you for your money and were modest to the point of being withdrawn. Besides, Higa would be almost thirty and she wouldn't be like a "grandma." Alex was already into his third cup of sake, so Tom chalked his opinions up to the drink.

"I've only known one Okinawan girl," Tom said cordially after making another effort to swallow some of the fiery sake, "and she was very nice to be with and to look at, but...but somehow I lost track of her."

"No problem, old man," the Wichitan laughed, nudging Tom's arm knowingly. "There's plenty more where she came from."

"Not like Higa. Her name was Higa. Did you ever

hear..." Tom looked at the grinning, blinking, increasingly drunk Alex and decided it was ridiculous to expect to get any information about Higa from him. "Let's get out of here," he said, almost crankily. "I'm hungry and this sake is about to kill both of us."

Alex jumped to his feet and said, "I know just the place. They have charcoaled steaks just like the Cattle King in Wichita."

Then he put his arm about Tom's shoulders, both as a friendly gesture and an attempt to steady himself, as the two men walked out of the little bar. Alex added confidently, "And we can get some good old rip-roarin' American whiskey to go with it."

Alex walked ahead aggressively, almost dragging Tom with him, weaving slightly from time to time along the shadowy street which was crowded with an assortment of uniformed Americans and comfortably dressed Okinawans. He would turn back frequently to make some comment to Tom about a shop they were passing or to get Tom's eyes to follow his, wolf-staring at some particularly well-developed Okinawan girl.

Finally, they came to a well-lit tea house known as The Gardens. A floorshow was in progress as they entered, and the glances from generally well-dressed, mostly Asian diners sent a shiver of embarrassment through Tom as he glanced down at his muddy, rumpled trousers and perspiration-wrinkled coat. He forgave Alex a little for bringing him to this place in his condition when he saw him heading for the cabaret located to the left of the entranceway, opposite the dining area.

Alex handed the bartender a bill and whispered an order into his ear. He turned then to Tom and, with a look of conniving accomplishment said, "We'll have a drink or two of real American whiskey just to whet our appetites before we eat."

In a low and confiding tone, he added, "American whiskey is hard to find, you know, except on the base."

Alex glanced about as though afraid someone would overhear him, then mumbled "unless you know somebody, of course."

Tom wasn't too impressed with Alex's "inside knowledge" but the friendly soldier seemed to enjoy divulging it so much, Tom felt an unexplainable urge to act even more stupid than he was about such matters in order to increase the importance of the information. There was such a convivial warmth about the big freckled face that made Tom want to go along with him in what ever he was doing or saying. If it had been anyone else he would have been completely bored with the routine.

"It pays to know the right people," Tom said, winking at the big smiling face.

Alex's smile broadened. "I've got a few connections—a man learns a few things over here in fourteen months."

He handed Tom one of the drinks the jaunty little bartender had brought. "I can get cigarettes for you, too, if you want 'em. They're hard to get outside the base, you know."

"I didn't know," Tom said, after taking a swallow of his drink. "I don't smoke."

It was good whiskey, but Tom really didn't want it. He was starving, and what he wanted was food, especially if it was as good as Alex described. He was no longer concerned about the condition of his clothes, even compared to the fine dress of the other diners. The happily clamoring sounds of eating utensils and voices taunted his stomach unmercifully. Still, he tried to keep the conversation flowing: "This is good whiskey, Alex, but tell me, how did you know they had it?"

"Good buddy, I know the old man that bootlegs it. He gets it out at the officer's club on the base. He used to work for the base until business got so good. Now he lives in Shuri—has the best house in town. He's a funny little feller—can't speak English real smooth and doesn't have much to say, but everybody likes him. We call him Hainju. His name means running water. Pretty good cover-up, eh? He's a runner alright, but he's not running water." He looked at Tom and giggled, apparently unaware of the flood of excited delight that Tom felt sweeping through him from his hair roots to his toe nails.

Hainju! Of course! Tom almost yelled the words out across the room in his surprised excitement. He had forgotten about old Hainju, the little dried-up man that used to push the wheelbarrows of food for Higa and "her people."

Hainju would know Higa's where-abouts better than anyone else in Okinawa! Of course! Why hadn't he thought of Hainju?

"Where does this Hainju live?" Tom asked, trying not to appear too interested for fear of raising Alex's concern.

"Hell's bells, I don't know!" the soldier shot back nonchalantly. "Let's get something to eat." He stepped away from the bar, wavering and slouching, in a semi-drunken stupor. Tom felt alarm rising within him. This devil would have to get drunk just as he was about to become useful, even necessary.

Tom followed Alex's weaving body through the tables of diners, ignoring the quick, disdainful glances that were thrown at them. He could not blame the sophisticated-appearing diners for the scorn they must have been feeling toward the out-of-place drunken soldier and the filthy civilian. Alex started to sit at an empty table almost in the center of the dining room, but Tom pulled him away from the chair and guided him to a smaller table in the darkened fringes of the eating area.

"It's a wonder they don't arrest this Hainju fellow," Tom said after they were seated and had turned in their order. He hoped to provoke some comment from the addled brain of the fat soldier that might lead him to

Hainju.

"Hell no," Alex said with a disdainful grin. "He has everybody on his side. Boy, he's got it—lives like a king, boy. He's got everything sewed up."

Then he sat up straight, suddenly, and slapped his hands on the table, opening his eyes wide as though a brilliant thought had worked its way through his alcohol-fogged mind. "I just thought of something!" He leaned far back in his chair and pulled his billfold from his pocket. Dramatically, he slipped a card from the wallet and handed it to Tom. "This is the kind of an operator old Hainju is, boy. Here's his card."

Tom took the card and laid it quickly on the table. He desperately wanted to avoid letting Alex see how his hand was trembling from excitement.

"Finest American Liquors-Whiskeys-Tobaccos," the card proclaimed. Under those words were Hainju's full name and address. Both the sake, whiskey and the thrill of suddenly gaining access to his beloved Higa were overwhelming! Tom could barely breathe.

He stuck the card hurriedly into his pocket and took a drink of water to attempt to hide what had to be showing in his face and eyes. All these days of empty searching were about to come to an end. He wanted to run out to his car and rush immediately to Hainju's house in Shuri.

The huge, expertly broiled steak arrived. Moments before he could hardly wait to devour the meal. Suddenly he couldn't bear to eat. He attempted several stabs at it with his knife and fork, but all he could think about was seeing Higa again.

Would she be as young and beautifully tender? As sweet and gracious? Would she love him still, as he loved her? Would she truly be able to share the secret of immortality? His mind raced.

Tom had difficulty waiting for Alex to finish. He watched the wolf-sized bites of steak disappear down the soldier's throat, afraid to speak lest he delay the consumption time. He almost shouted "No!" when the waiter asked him if he cared for dessert. He knew his impatience was too transparent when the waiter showed considerable concern when he saw that Tom had barely touched the steak.

"The food is fine," Tom said over and over. "I just wasn't hungry." Alex merely stared at him incongruously.

Tom left a five dollar tip and paid the check. The young Okinawan waiter was still bowing as they walked out the door.

"I've got some important business matters to attend to and it's getting late," Tom said, hoping to explain his sudden anxiousness to be on his way.

"Sure, Tom. I've stayed past curfew anyway." He laughed as though he had told a joke. Tom laughed with him, relieved that he was ready to go, too. He wasn't surprised when Alex readily accepted a ride back to the Kadena Air Base. It would delay him in getting back to Shuri but, after all, a little delay was nothing compared to the invaluable information the soldier had given him quite by accident.

Alex talked all the way back to his base and didn't seem aware that Tom wasn't listening to a word he was saying. Alex's words flew by Tom's thoughts. There was nothing he wanted to hear or that he could comprehend at the moment except the prospect of seeing Hainju, then Higa. He could almost see the darting black eyes of old Hainju, and he could almost feel Higa's hand in his. He had no trouble visualizing Higa's full red lips, tugging down at the corners. The thoughts rushed over him as the car's headlights illuminated the highway ahead.

A few moments later, Tom was shaking hands with Alex and telling him goodbye, perhaps a bit too casually, considering the importance of the information Alex had unwittingly given him.

Alex got out of the car quickly, leaving only a patch of darkness in the night to replace his face. Soon the automobile was speeding furtively toward Shuri.

Tom was familiar with the residential area that surrounded the University of the Ryukus where Hainju lived. Earlier, during the first few days in Okinawa, he had even taken a few walks through the area in his attempts to find her.

Now, he had little difficulty in finding the right street, even though there were no street lights and most houses appeared to have been darkened for the night. Hainju's house was easy to identify, for it had a tile roof, a mark of distinction in Okinawa. It also stood out like a shiny, new-minted coin amidst its neighbor's thatch-roofed houses. It had large gardens all about with neatly trimmed shrubs and exquisitely cared-for flowers whose colors seemed rich and bright even in the half light of the moon.

Tom sat in his car blinking at the house and its elegant surroundings in awe. The insignificant pusher of a wheelbarrow lived there? Could it be true that the skinny Hainju lived in that house? Tom let the motor of his rented car run while he debated whether to go on in now and risk arousing Hainju from his sleep, thus possibly alienating him as an informant of Higa's whereabouts, or waiting until morning.

Then the memory of Hainju's thin smile came to him. The old man was far too good-natured to refuse him even at this late hour. Tom shut off the motor and opened the car door, cringing at its noisy squeaking. He walked up the stone, flower-bordered walk and knocked at the door, timidly at first, then with more vigor.

Finally a tall, heavy-stomached man opened the door

with a quick, sweeping motion and glared at Tom. The man completely blocked the doorway. His small eyes seemed almost to glow in the dim light, and his somber face reflected wariness and distrust. He looked more like a guard than a butler.

"Name?" he asked after a moment of staring at Tom. Apparently the man at least knew some English.

"I'm an old friend of Hainju," Tom said with as much conviviality as he could muster, wishing at the same time that he had waited until morning to call on Hainju. "I'm Tom Bristow—from America." His words seemed lost in the quaint, darkened house.

The distrusting oriental was thoroughly unimpressed. Tom fought the despair that gathered in his throat. He stared at the big curving lips silently for a moment, then he barked with as much authority as he could muster, "Show me to Hainju! Now!"

The man never blinked: "Hainju very sick. Nobody see him—doctor say." His eyes were quickly diverted to the roll of American currency Tom had suddenly thought to pull out of his pocket. The curved lips straightened into almost a smile as the butler took the money quickly and motioned Tom to follow him. He walked soundlessly down a carpeted, dimly lighted hallway until they came to a closed door at the far end.

"Please remove shoes," the oriental whispered. "Hainju there." He motioned with his head toward the door, then bowed stiffly and walked back down the hall fondling the bills as he went.

Tom took off his shoes and moved quickly, anxious to do whatever was necessary to see the only person he knew that could tell him where to find Higa.

He opened the door slowly, half fearful and completely enthralled at the prospects before him. From what Alex had told him, Hainju would be sitting in purple robes on a throne-like chair with servants standing nearby, ready to carry out his orders. Therefore, Tom was entirely unprepared for the unattended and pitiful appearance of his host.

Hainju was propped up in his bed, his eyes closed as if asleep, all alone. His sallow skin looked as though someone had draped it over a pile of bones. Tom walked quietly to the side of the bed where he lay and peered down at the yellowed and drawn features. It was definitely Hainju, but not the quick, cheery wheelbarrow-pusher he remembered.

"Hainju," Tom whispered softly.

The old man's eyelids opened hesitantly and his black eyes stared at Tom with no sign of recognition. After a moment of dull staring, the wrinkled lids closed and Tom felt his hopes of ever finding Higa fading. This withered and wasting lump of flesh was his last thin fiber of hope—the last groping chance he had of finding Higa and her secret of immortality.

Tom bent down close and fought to avoid flinching at the foul breath. "Hainju! Do you remember me? I'm Tom Bristow—American G. I. Remember?"

He waited for a response. Nothing.

Tom continued urgently—"A long time ago I helped you get food for your people. You pushed the food in your wheelbarrow for me and Higa."

Hainju's eyes opened slowly at the sound of Higa's name and his sunken face smiled briefly.

"Higa," he said in a low, rattling voice. "Higa..." He halted and looked up at the ceiling as though speaking and even remembering were too severe of an effort.

Tom watched the thin lips. Inwardly, he hoped and prayed. Suddenly he was stricken with the idea that Anna would have prayed, too, in this situation.

"God keep him alive—keep him alive long enough."

Tom was surprised at how easily and naturally the silent words came to him. Anna would have been proud of him. Then his thoughts switched back quickly to Hainju as the old man's lips fluttered. Words, barely audible, rattled around in his throat.

"I am old man now—and so sick. I remember you Tom—good man. Higa love you so mu..."

His voice broke and he sighed heavily. He reached a skinny hand out to Tom and continued in a high, quavering voice.

"Sit, Tom. I am old. There are few that seek me out anymore unless they want whiskey. Welcome to my home."

Tom took the old man's hand in his and sat down beside the bed. It appeared that he was suffering from acute hepatitis but he couldn't be sure. "If I were a doctor and had equipment and drugs and time I could help him," he reflected, but there was no point in thinking of that now. Something much more important than that was at hand. He must learn of Higa's whereabouts before Hainju became incoherent.

"Hainju, you remember Higa, the girl you spoke of? I have come back from America to find her. I must find her. Do you understand?"

He waited for Hainju to answer but the wrinkled eyelids closed again. The ancient man seemed unaware of anything Tom was saying. Tom leaned closer to the yellow face and the stinking breath, trying desperately to speak more clearly, "I must find Higa! I need her very much. Do you hear me? Can you tell me where I can find her?"

He waited for the words he wanted desperately to hear, watching the thin lips for any sign of movement or direction. It was like trying to make a dream turn out the way one wanted, but waking up before the dream was over.

"I will pay you whatever you ask or do whatever you want done. Please tell me, Hainju. Tell me if you know."

Tom tried to restrain the feeling of impatience and anger that was welling up within him. He put his hand on the old man's shoulder and shook him lightly, urgently asking, "Do you hear me, Hainju?"

Hainju opened his eyes slowly and spoke with surprising calmness, as though he had now gathered together enough strength to talk: "I have no need of your money. I am rich man. I have doctor. I have tutor to teach me better English. I have servants..."

A long pause followed. Then just as quickly as he stopped talking, he began again in mid-sentence: "...but I have sick body and none of it is good now. None can help me now."

His eyes closed again and the yellow face seemed to fade into an almost colorless, bloodless gray. Tom despaired of ever getting any sense out of this delirious old man. He thought of the long years he had kept Higa and her secret of immortality hidden away in the nethermost part of his mind, sometimes trying to rid himself of it as though it were a disease. At other times he had literally pulled the memory out into the light of reality to analyze it and test it for flaws. The obsession had fluctuated back and forth, from fondled hope to shameful secrecy. Now he was finally so close to finding the answer, yet it was buried so deeply in Hainju's rotting brain cells that Tom might never know. He bowed his head in his hand and held his lips to muffle the choking chagrin that filled his throat.

There must be something he could do to shock the old man into reviving himself long enough to speak with coherence and sanity. Tom grabbed the old man's shoulders impulsively and shook him vigorously. "Tell me where Higa is!" He yelled in as loud a voice as he dared use in deference to the butler and the other servants in the house, then in a lower tone, he added, "and I will give you the secret to immortality!"

Hainju's eyes opened once again and a half smile revealed his teeth, yellowed and crooked. The old man spoke with more strength than at any other time since

Tom had been there.

"You speak as my mother did long ago."

Hainju paused, his eyes brighter, as though thinking of her invigorated him.

"She used to tell me that our people were happy immortals..." He paused again and Tom thought he heard a low chuckle in his throat. The old man continued hoarsely, "...but she was wrong—just as wrong as you are wrong. I must die—just as she died."

He turned his head and rolled his eyes over, to look directly at Tom as though searching for understanding. He coughed and then looked back up at the ceiling as though content with what he has said.

"No, Hainju, you are mistaken," Tom said, pitying him for his ignorance and hopelessness. "I promise you, Higa knows. She'll give us both her secret to immortality if you can tell me where she is."

Hainju looked at Tom for a moment, then with a sigh of resignation, he said "You are foolish man, Tom. You look too long for trouble." He looked back up at the ceiling and his eyes misted over for a moment before he resumed his hoarse whispering. Tom leaned forward, straining to hear every word.

"Higa wait many months and years for you with much hope. Each night she go and stand on hill where she knew you. But you never come back."

Tom's heart swelled with pride at the thought of Higa's long years of loyalty to him. Then the pride faded into shame when he thought of how she must have finally started hating him as the years went by and he never returned. Hainju's words stabbed his heart mercilessly.

"Where is she now, Hainju? Where is she now?" he asked impatiently.

"Higa's father was bad man—like me. Worse even. He had place in the Neusegua. He try all time to get Higa to make him much money. She beautiful and soldiers like very much to have her. But she good woman. Higa never give in."

His voice died down to an inaudible sigh but he smiled and looked at the ceiling as though savoring with great relish his thoughts of Higa. Tom wanted to urge him on, to force him to keep talking. Yet he dared not press the old man too far.

"Higa wait for you each night." Hainju finally continued. "She watch the sea. She hope…"

There was another long pause and Tom took a handkerchief from his pocket and swabbed at the tears that had collected in the boney eye-sockets and at the sweat that stood in the furrows of his forehead. Hainju smiled appreciatively.

"One night big typhoon wave come and Higa is gone. People see it sweep her from hill into the sea and she is gone. Many others gone."

The tears filled the sunken eye-sockets again. "She had to die—just as I must die. Is NO secret to immortality…"

Tom drew back from the stench of Hainju's breath. He looked at the grizzly lips and tried to absorb the sounds they had just uttered. He wanted to shake the boney throat until it swallowed up the incomprehensible words that Hainju had just spoken. Tom wanted to believe they were the outpourings of a sick and fevered brain. Inwardly, however, he knew the old man had told him the truth. The grief in his eyes was unmistakable. Higa was gone forever.

She had been wrong about her claim to immortality. There was no doubt about it now. The crazy illusion was gone. Worse, the pursuit of her, and it, had now cost him years of needless pondering. It had cost him his medical degree. It had cost him any hope of a relationship with his father. It had perhaps cost him Anna,too. He shuddered at the thoughts that swept over him, wave after wave, and wiped his eyes that had suddenly filled with scalding tears.

The old man sighed, long and heavily, as though relieved to share his sad knowledge of Higa, seemingly unaware that Tom had risen to his feet.

"Thank you for telling me the truth about Higa," Tom said, straining unsuccessfully to keep his voice from breaking. "I'll always remember and love her."

Bending low over the wrinkled face, he asked, "Is there anything I can do for you, Hainju?"

Old Hainju held his hand up with great effort and, smiling feebly, said, "No, Tom. I have good doctor—and all that money can buy. I live a little while longer, then I go the way of my fathers. Just remember me sometimes, Tom."

Tom held the soft decaying hand for just a moment, then laid it gently across the shallow stomach and left, looking back briefly at the helpless, wrinkled figure.

"I'll remember you, Hainju." Tom said wistfully, knowing it would undoubtedly be the last time he would ever see the old man alive. "I'll remember…"

After leaving Hainju's house, Tom spent three days wandering all over the island, remembering a soldier's life there that seemed eons ago. On the final evening, he went to the hill where Higa had stood so many times, waiting for him. It was the hill where she had been washed out to sea and lost forever.

He took the magatama out of his pocket, fingered the sparkling, curved green and black striped gem for a few moments, then he tossed the jeweled keepsake into the crashing waves below. Tossed by the surf momentarily, the gem and its chain swirled in the rushing water, then sank from sight, gone forever.

"Goodbye," he whispered to the rocks and waves below. "Goodbye, Higa. I will hold you in my heart forever.

Goodbye, my love."

The front-desk clerk at the Rican Hotel directed Tom to a downtown office where he could send a Western Union telegram. The next day, a dispatcher from Guymon delivered a familiar-looking yellow paper to Bejamin Bristow:

BEEN IN OKINAWA HEADING HOME TOMORROW STOP WILL EXPLAIN WHEN I ARRIVE TOM

The plane's engines throbbed with exuberance as the silver wings cut sharply into the late August air. The asphalt runway flashed close beneath them for a moment and then gave way to a broad greenness of trees and hillsides which grew smaller and smaller until it formed the long, narrow strip of an island that is Okinawa. Tom watched it disappear in a mixture of sea and distance and he felt as though a weight as big as the island itself had left him and been tossed into the waves below.

The droning of the motors sounded almost musical. They seemed to be singing, beating out words of freedom for him. It had taken several days to reach this point.

He was free now, free from Higa and free from Anna, free from school and free from Benjamin and the Hawk Ranch. He was free from all the ties that ever held him. There was nothing now but the hum of the plane's engines.

He had no decisions about whether to recommend surgery or not, where to make the critical incision, no fretting about immortality, no worries about how to get along with his father, no more difficulties with Anna and her mother. He was free to float along, as he was now doing.

He would return to the Hawk Ranch to gather his things, then he would find a way to discover what he was really meant to do.

Maybe, of all the people he had met, Judge Anson and Jeanie had the right idea—live, love, laugh, and leave. Tom grinned, then his smile broadened as he thought of Jeanie, her dancing eyes and her warm body on the number five fairway. He reclined his airplane chair back as far as it would go. Its upholstered curves were soft and comforting.

He was landing in Amarillo. He had parked his convertible at a lot near the airport, which wasn't far from the judge's office. Before making the drive to Guymon and the Hawk Ranch, he would visit the judge and Jeanie.

"It'll be great to see them again," he mused wistfully, unsurprised at the inner stirring, "especially Jeanie."

Robert Boyd Delano

12

Jeanie's hair was piled high on her head in an austere bouffant, and her eyes were painted too dimly blue. Still, the artist had caught the tease in her smile perfectly. The oil portrait was mostly impressive because it covered most of the entire north wall of Judge Jacob Anson's darkly paneled outer office.

"Judge Anson will see you in a moment, sir," his secretary said, sweeping her hazel eyes across Tom in a cold, professional, evaluating glance. She motioned to a chair beside a stack of magazines on a table. Tom noticed that she resumed filing her nails.

Tom glanced briefly at the offered chair but decided his best view of Jeanie's portrait was from where he was presently standing. Jeanie was agonizingly bewitching even in the still life that the artist had painted. He looked from the portrait to the judge's closed door and wished there were some way he could hurry the judge into coming out of his office. He had to get the judge to take him to Jeanie now, to convert the cold, unmoving brush strokes into the vivacious, warm, dancing, sensuous Jeanie with whom he had shared unforgettable moments on the Hawk Ranch number five fairway.

It seemed like an hour before Judge Anson's office door popped open suddenly and his voluminous, earth-shaped body appeared through the door.

"Tommy Bristow! This is a pleasant surprise." He rushed forward with his hand outstretched. "Sorry to keep you waiting—I thought I'd never get off the phone. Of course, if you have to wait, I always say there's no better place to wait than in Amarillo, Texas." He laughed diaphragmatically.

"I didn't mind waiting, at all," Tom lied, shaking the plump hand vigorously and nodding at the huge portrait. "Of course, I'd like to see her in person, too. I tried to phone from the airport when I flew into town an hour or so ago, but I couldn't rouse anyone at your home."

The judge laughed, looking away from his daughter's portrait quickly as though he had just thought of some urgent, interfering matter.

"She can wait," he said. "It's been a tough day."

He was exasperated and made no effort to mask his feelings, heaving a gigantic sigh through his heavy lips. He gave his secretary a quick, almost anxious glance. "I'm leaving for the day, Wanda."

Wanda was no longer filing her nails. Instead, perhaps for appearances in front of her boss, she was fidgeting with papers at her typewriter.

"Yessir, Judge Anson," she said absently, not looking up. "I'll see you tomorrow. I'll have these briefs on your desk when you arrive in the morning." She gave her typewriter carriage a quick push and began click-clacking at a frenetic pace.

Tom followed the judge out the door and had to hustle to keep pace with him as they walked together down the sidewalk. Wind tugged at their clothes and the late afternoon sun was blindingly bright. Tom was perplexed at Judge Anson's abrupt, dismissing comments concerning Jeanie back in his office. The judge had always gone out of his way to promote a closer relationship between his daughter and Tom. After puzzling over it for several moments, Tom finally attributed the judge's attitude to his obviously-tough day. However, he couldn't restrain himself from wondering what was happening.

"How is that fun-loving daughter of yours, Judge Anson? It seems like a year since I've seen her."

The judge suddenly turned, almost as if Tom had shoved him, and pushed his way through a glass door into a bar. He held the door open and gestured for Tom to follow. "Let's have a quick one before dinner, Tom. Good for the digestive juices, you know—especially if you've been hitting it hard all day."

The darkness of the bar's interior was more blinding than the brightness of the sidewalk and Tom had difficulty seeing his way to follow Judge Anson's huge figure as he led him back through a maze of scattered, silent-huddled patrons. The judge finally selected a leatherette-upholstered booth and slid into it, his stomach completely filling all available space. Tom felt the table move toward him a little as he sat down on the opposite side.

"Been wanting to try this new place," the judge said when they were finally settled. It was obvious he was purposefully ignoring Tom's inquiries concerning Jeanie. Tom felt a strange mixture of anger and curiosity coursing through his brain. He could hardly wait until the waiter took their order so he could probe deeper.

"Is Jeanie about ready to start back at the University of Texas?" Tom asked, trying to sound pleasant.

"No, apparently she's not going back to UT this fall." The judge looked impatiently toward the bar and slapped the top of the table loudly. "It takes these donkey's rear-ends an hour to fix a little drink in here." He turned to Tom and said less noisily, "That's what comes from trying something new. Should have stuck to Jakes."

"What do you mean, she won't be going back this fall? What is she going to do?"

The drinks came and the judge tossed his down before the waiter was out of sight.

"You're a nosey young sprout, Tom, but I guess you're

entitled to know. Besides you'd find out anyway." Judge Anson paused and drew a long, quivering breath. "Jeanie up and ran off with a professional wrestler about two weeks ago. He wasn't a very good wrestler even, just a big, bulky beast with a lot of hair on his chest." He wiped at his lips with the back of his hand and stared at his empty glass, unquestionably and uncontrollably vanquished by an unseen foe.

"He filled her head with tales about making it big in California," the judge added. "She jumped in his old beat-up Cadillac one day and off they went. There wasn't anything I could do about it, short of shooting the guy, and I thought of doin' that."

"Did they get married or...?" Tom asked, after a few reeling moments of trying to bring his shocked senses into focus. He knew Jeanie was a free spirit, but taking off for California with an almost total stranger seemed a little too free.

"I really can't say—and I'm not sure I want her to get married to the ape. It's a horrible lot for her either way. She's so young—so foolish, Tom. She didn't have any more sense than an over-sexed grasshopper."

Tom felt a storm of resentment gathering within him. What right did that hairy-chested monster have to run away with a sweet, gullible, young girl like Jeanie? A girl he had only known a couple of weeks? He ordered another drink with the judge.

"He had no right to her," Tom said, realizing the second he spoke the words that the wrestler had as much right to her as he did, and probably as much hope of getting her to settle down. He almost laughed at the irony of it. He had come back for the same purpose as the wrestler—to enjoy a pleasurable encore with Jeanie. But the wrestler had beat him to it and whisked her away to the Golden State. It was another total loss. The flames of the whiskey licked at his throat as he tipped the glass all the way up. He might as well rack Jeanie up alongside the others; she belonged with all the other lost ones—his mother, Anna, Higa, Benjamin and even the failed medical degree at the University of Saint Louis. Add sweet Jeanie to the list.

"You don't know how it hurts me, Tom. And it takes a hell of a lot to hurt me, too."

"Yes, I know judge. I think I know how it hurts."

Tom obviously didn't know how it would hurt to lose an only daughter, but he had known loss, painful loss. Again and again.

Someone clanked a coin in the jukebox. Billy Eckstine's unmistakeable voice began:

> The night is like a lovely tune
> Beware my foolish heart
> How white the ever constant moon
> Take care my foolish heart

"I've gotta go," Tom said suddenly, starting to get up.

"Wait, Tom. Wait a moment. Let's have one more. I've been so lonesome since Jeanie left. Let's drink a toast to Jeanie."

> There's a line between love and fascination
> That's hard to see on an evening such as this
> For they both give the very same sensation
> When you're lost in the magic of a kiss
> Her lips are much too close to mine
> Beware my foolish heart

The judge waved his huge, white-sleeved arm at the waiter and Tom sat back down as he thought he saw a tear rolling down the judge's face. Then the moving green light of the jukebox swept the older man's large shaking jowls and Tom could see clearly the wet path of the tear. He was a sad and lonely man. He had lost his daughter, just as Tom had lost her, only a million times more painfully. But, at least, the judge still had something; he still had his prestigious career to keep him company. That, and whiskey.

For this time it isn't fascination
Or a dream that will fade and fall apart
It's love, this time it's love
My foolish heart

"To Jeanie," Tom said, clinking his glass against the barrister's upheld glass. "To Jeanie, the girl who knows how to live, love, laugh and leave.

"That's good, Tom," Judge Anson remarked appreciatively. "Live, love, laugh and leave. I like that."

Even as he said the words, the judge stared at his drink intently. In that moment, his face seemed to age ten years; the jowls sagged and the lines in his face deepened as he sat shaking his head. Tears began rolling like huge, white-hot rain drops down his massive cheeks. Judge Anson made no attempt to hide the tears. Some of them splashed on the table and glistened brightly in the green light.

"Actually," he said sadly, his voice quivering, "it's not true at all, Tom. Life has to be more than just living, loving, laughter, and leaving. She'll learn someday—she'll find it out the hard way as we all must."

"Find out what?" Tom asked, finishing his drink.

"It's not about living it up. Not all the time, anyway. Sure, I believe in having fun, but most of the time I'm working my butt off so we can afford to have a nice life. It's not always about fun. It's a lot of things. Life can be a whole hell of a lot of serious things, too. Jeanie'll find out after about a month with that hairy-chested hunk of muscle that he's not the answer to everything. And she'll find out that California isn't the magical place she thinks it will be."

The older man shook his head. He laughed bitterly. "I'm sorry, Tom. I'm boring you. And I'm embarrassing myself. Blame it on the whiskey, but it's true."

"I want to hear what you're saying," Tom urged. "If it's not about laughter and having a good time, what is it? I've often wondered about the really important things in life..."

"That's because no one knows the answer."

"No one?"

"Maybe," the judge replied. Then he shrugged weakly—"I don't know. There have been times in my life when I thought I had the answers. I don't feel that way now."

They sat for a moment looking blankly at each other. The silence between them made the clamor of the juke box unbearable.

"I've got to be going now, Judge Anson. I..."

"Where you going, Tom?" The older man squinted at him as though trying to hold Tom to his chair with his eyes.

"Home."

"Back to the Hawk Ranch?"

"Yeah. I'm going to stop at Guymon one more time, then go to the Hawk Ranch. That's the only home I've got for right now. But I think it's about time I started figuring out what I need to do with my life."

"Well, hell, let's have one more together, Tom. We'll drink to Benjamin and the Hawk Ranch." Judge Anson raised his hand to wave the waiter over, but Tom stood up.

"No. I've really got to go now. Please let me drop you off at your house first. Then I've got to go home."

Night had enveloped Amarillo by the time Tom stopped his convertible in front of the judge's stately brick home. He helped the older man inside.

"Stay the night," the judge offered. "Benjamin would shoot me if he knew I let you drive all the way to Guymon this late. And as you can tell, I've got plenty of empty bedrooms. Take your pick of any damned one."

It did make sense, so Tom decided to stay. He fell into one of the guest beds completely exhausted.

Judge Anson seemed in a better mood the next morning. The two men enjoyed a quick breakfast at a busy diner, then Tom dropped the barrister off at his office and pointed the maroon Ford north toward Guymon.

13

Indian Summer shimmered invitingly as Tom drove into Guymon. The last two miles, as he approached the outskirts of the small town, looked the best of all. It was as though the Oklahoma Panhandle had put on its finest apparel to welcome one of its natives home. Broad fields lay plowed and proud, proclaiming eloquently that they were not ashamed to turn themselves wrong-side-out each year for all the world to view. Pastures languished serene and confident, as if they were satisfied with what they had accomplished during the past growing season. For this moment, Tom felt closer to this land than to any living soul.

In fact, he felt so good he decided to stop and see Anna. Perhaps she would have missed him and run to him with open arms. Perhaps he would say a final goodbye. Or maybe...? He forced the thought of a reunion out of his mind.

Dr. Taylor came to the door. He seemed surprised beyond words, then opened the door and offered his hand. Anna's father seemed grim and even more formal than usual. Tom supposed it was due to having his sermon preparations interrupted.

"I'm sorry to interfere with your studies, Dr. Taylor," Tom began, struggling to explain his absence. "I've been out of the country a few weeks. Is Anna here? I'd like to see her for a moment."

The younger man smiled, hoping to hide his uneasiness. "I suppose Anna is doing her usual Saturday morning grocery shopping."

Suddenly, instinctively, he sensed something horribly wrong, inexorably changed. Tom felt a shiver run the length of his spine.

"Come inside, Tom," Dr. Taylor asked evenly. "We need to talk."

Without further greeting, the parson turned and walked toward his study. Tom followed, noticing as they walked through the front room that something seemed very different. The study looked the same as always; the same orderly but often-referred-to shelves of books, the same worn linoleum and dim drapes. Dr. Taylor stopped at his desk and looked with preoccupied soberness at what appeared to be the half-written sermon he would deliver the next day. Tom remained standing, waiting.

"I tried to locate you, Tom, but they said you had gone on a long vacation trip."

Now it was the pastor who was obviously struggling for words. Inexplicably, he was also struggling to contain his emotions.

"Apparently you haven't heard...," his voice faltered and he looked at Tom with a sadness in his eyes that Tom had never seen there before. Tom's uneasiness grew.

"Heard about what?"

Dr. Taylor finished his question, "You haven't heard about Anna?" He stared at Tom, the sadness brimming his eyes. "Tom, Anna is gone. She passed away almost a week ago."

"Anna? Dead?" Tom whispered the words half aloud as if it were necessary to speak them out loud to believe they had ever been uttered.

"Anna? Dead?" He said it again. Such strange words. Yes, people died all the time, but not Anna. This was something incongruent and unacceptable. His legs collapsed under him. He sank into a chair. His face felt clammy, and the room whirled around him. Hot droplets of tears slid down his cheeks, then splashed onto the clean linoleum floor.

For an eternity, it seemed, he wept uncontrollably. Then he felt Dr. Taylor's hand on his shoulder and after a few moments he heard the old minister say, "It's okay to grieve, son. Just don't grieve for Anna. She's far happier now than she ever was in this life."

The pastor's words made no sense. Anna had always been the happiest girl in the world. Even during the worst times with her mother, she was the one who cheered up everyone. How could death be happier?

"Anna is at home with her mother now," the minister's gentle, stern voice continued. "She's at home with Jesus. And it's a joyful place—a home for happy immortals, I'd say."

Tom raised his head and looked at Dr. Taylor. The words happy immortals slashed like knife blades at his insides. He had heard the phrase before so many times, but it wasn't true. Higa had proven that. Hainju had said so. The irony of any mention of immortality seemed so cruel and out of place in the midst of death.

"How can she be happy now?" Tom's grief exploded from somewhere deep inside. "She's not immortal. She's gone! Forever!"

Dr. Taylor's hand remained on Tom's shoulder, but he spoke no words, listening as Tom's heart overflowed with grief.

"What a waste!" Tom thought. "What a futile, foolish waste. Anna and I could have been together all these wasted years—married and happy."

Tom looked at Dr. Taylor through rivulets of tears—"I

loved her. I loved her all those years. You know that—but she quit loving me. Something happened, and she quit loving me." He put his hands to his eyes and tried to stop the hot flow of tears but they kept pouring out, rolling and splashing downward.

"That's not true, Tom. Anna talked to me about you often. She always confided in me—she told me about it every time you asked her to marry you." Dr. Taylor smiled, an amused chuckle dying in his throat. "She wanted marriage more than anything but she felt a duty to stay with her mother as long as she lived. I always respected her for that—and I think you did, too."

"But why did she tell me it was too late?" Tom shot back. "She told me she loved me, but it was too late."

The pastor hesitated, looking directly into Tom's face. He seemed to struggle for the right words to say. Finally, taking a deep breath, he began: "Six months ago, even as she watched her mother going downhill, Ann was diagnosed with cancer..."

"But why didn't she tell me?" Tom strained to keep from screaming the words. "She could have told me?"

"I wanted her to," Dr. Taylor said evenly. "I begged her to tell you. I told her she owed it to you. In the end, after all the years of watching her mother waste away, she made a very deliberate decision to make sure you didn't have to see her that way. She wanted you to live your own life. She didn't want to be a burden to you. Can you understand that now, Tom?"

"No!" Tom shouted. "Hell, no!" He realized that he shouldn't be cursing in front of a preacher, but nothing seemed to matter anymore. How could there be rules or order when everything he had ever wanted in life had been jerked away?

"When she first found out, you were still in medical school. She didn't want it to interfere with your studies. Then, after you quit school," Dr. Taylor looked away from Tom as though embarrassed to mention it, "and after you asked her to marry you the last time, she didn't want to handicap you, to have you marry a cripple, as she put it."

"She thought she'd be a hindrance to me? My God. What a fool I've been—not to know what was happening to her and to me too." Then, giving vent to the anger within him, he said, "Why didn't the doctor do something for her."

"He did. Dr. Rongern was very helpful. But Anna's condition had gone too far to do much about it. No one anticipated how aggressive the cancer would be."

Dr. Taylor seemed to want to say more, but he choked on the final sentence. Only then did Tom realize that he had been so focused on his own hurt and pain that he hadn't remotely considered how much unbearable, unspeakable grief the pastor had experienced in the loss of both his wife and daughter.

Dr. Taylor sat at his desk and wiped his eyes. Tom stared at the floor. He wanted to bolt from the room and run toward his waiting convertible. He wanted to speed away and forget these horrible moments. Instead, his feet felt as if they were welded to the floor. His heart had turned to stone.

After several minutes the pastor regained his composure enough to reach inside the middle desk drawer. He pulled a simple envelope from inside and handed it to Tom.

"I don't know when she wrote this, but on the last day she was alive, Anna asked me to give it to you."

The two men looked at each other as men do when they seem to run out of words. Then Dr. Taylor finally spoke, "I know that many of her thoughts during her life were of you, especially toward the end of her life."

"I should have been here," Tom's anguished words spilled out. "I've ruined so many things. I've wasted so many years of my life. I wasted Anna's, too. And there's not a damn thing to show for it." Tom swallowed, resentiment heavy in his throat.

"You're wrong, Tom." The pastor spoke gently but sternly. "You have no idea how much you meant to Anna. And to her mother and me. Only time will tell you how much God has blessed you. You are just beginning to find out what He has given you. Anna knew. She knew more about things like that than most people I've ever met. And I pray that you will find out what He wants to do in your life."

Tom stood. He didn't want to be rude, but the last thing he wanted at the moment was a sermon about God.

"I need to be by myself for awhile," he told Dr. Taylor, who also rose. "Maybe we can talk about this sometime." He knew it was a lie. He never wanted to talk about death and life. He only wanted to get away. Even the Hawk Ranch seemed a haven at the moment.

"I'd like that," the parson said, referring to Tom's desire to talk in the future. "You will always be like a son to me. I give you my word that I will be lifting you up to the Lord every day. God knows what you are going through, and He cares for you more than you will ever know."

The Ford flathead V-8 roared mercilessly. Tom's thoughts were jumbled. He strained to see through his tears. He couldn't see the speedometer or how fast he was going, nor did he care.

"God knows what I'm going through?" he asked mockingly into the prairie air as he sped on the road. "He cares for me?"

Inwardly, he seethed. He railed against God, Dr. Taylor, Anna, Higa, Jeanie, his father, Judge Anson, his mother. All he had ever known had been a horrible, terrible lie. What a waste his life had been? Everything he had touched seemed to corrode and dissolve.

He floored the accelerator, caring less and less whether he lived or died. Worse, he felt no one else cared. By some stroke of fortune, he survived the curves, tires screeching and gravel flying, and sped toward the only home he had really ever known.

Robert Boyd Delano

14

Harriett shouted from the back door as Tom started walking from his car to the house. "Hurry, Tom! Something awful is happening to Mr. Bristow! The door to his office is locked. He's being hurt. Thank God you're here!"

Her face was blanched white and her lips quivered in terror as she motioned frantically for him to hurry.

"I've called the sheriff's office!" she screamed. "They're on their way, but you've got to do something now before he kills your father!"

"He?"

His thoughts raced as he tried to figure out what she was talking about. Harriett's fear pulled at Tom like a magnet and he darted past her, sensing from her wild, speechless gesturing that the "awful happening" was in Benjamin's office. In the split second it took him to reach the door he became aware of an ominous presence inside the house.

Behind the locked office door, he heard the sounds of scuffling feet, the crashing of wood against metal and flesh against flesh pounded at his ears. It was like the meat-smashing noises that Willie Lusby's fists had made against the skinny Jenning's face that day behind Lonnie's pool hall. Tom, above it all, though, heard the horror stricken screams of Harriett as she ran behind him through the dining room.

"He's gonna to kill him! Ohmigawd, he's gonna to kill him."

Tom crashed against the locked door. The heavy wood splintered and the door burst open just as Benjamin flew backward through the room, his arms spread out like the wings of a soaring hawk. The full force of his body slammed against the sharp corner of a filing cabinet and he sprawled to the floor, crumpling like a dropped scarf. The filing cabinet vibrated a second against the wall and then all was quiet except for hoarse breathing from across the room which Tom heard now for the first time. He knew who it was before he turned to look. Willie Lusby stood only a few feet away, crouching, fists still clinched, his shirt wet with perspiration, the heavy face a purple-grey as his thick lips alternated between leering and grimly sucking air.

"Get up, you skinny old bird, if you want some more," the bully said between gasps of air.

Benjamin's body lay very still but he turned his head toward Tom. Benjamin's eyelids fluttered open. He looked at Tom in a helpless mixture of anger and fear.

"I can't move my legs, Tom!" the rancher cried hoarsely. "He's taking my money, and I can't do anything about it. Help me, son!"

Tom followed Benjamin's eyes to the safe where Willie stood. At his feet were fat bundles of currency taken from the safe and stuffed hurriedly into a canvas bag.

Terror seized at all of Tom's insides as he thought of the bloody face of the skinny one. It could happen to him, just as it had happened to Jennings. He could almost feel Willie's heavy fists crashing into his face.

Tom was vaguely aware of Harriett's soft sobs as she still stood in frozen despair by the doorway.

"Put the money back, Willie," Tom heard himself saying. He was almost startled by the steely sound coming from inside his throat

Willie peered at Tom with a puzzled, irritated face that quickly melted into a leering gloat.

"Whadju say, kid?" Willie grinned tauntingly.

"It's over, Willie." Tom struggled to keep his voice from cracking. He couldn't let his fear show. "The sheriff is almost here. Put the money back in the safe. You're not going anywhere except to prison."

Willie's fists clinched but his lips continued to leer as he shouted—"And you can go straight to hell!"

His lips suddenly lost their looseness, tightening against the horsey teeth. The first onrush of fists came like thunderbolts, but Tom ducked quickly. Willie almost fell but recovered his balance. For an instant he glared at Tom with hate-filled eyes, then the taunting grin returned.

"I almost forgot," Willie said, letting his arms drop to his side for a moment. "You're the boy with no guts. You didn't even stick up for poor old Jennings down at Lonnie's Place. Why don't you run along and play now while I get back to more important things."

"No, Willie! You're not taking Dad's money, and you're going to pay for a long time what you've done to my Dad." Tom felt his throat tighten as he spoke.

"I'm just taking what I'm entitled to."

Willie's protruding teeth showed through the fat lips again.

"You're gonna have to walk over my dead body to leave here before the sheriff arrives," Tom said. He saw the hate rising in Willie's eyes.

"I'm gonna enjoy doing that," Willie shot back.

Tom wiped the sweat from his eyes as he waited for the onslaught.

In the background, he heard the wailing siren of the sheriff's car. Willie heard it, too. Suddenly, Willie turned into a cornered animal with absolutely nothing to lose.

Willie swung so viciously, Tom heard him grunt with the effort. Blinding light exploded inside Tom's skull and he felt himself swaying under a quick volley of blows. They came in rapid succession to both sides of his face. Tom dropped to one knee, partly from necessity and partly to avoid the flailing fists. He could feel blood gushing down his face. He opened his eyes and for an instant saw the black staring eyes of his father, full of agony—a lost, spiritless, distraught stare.

"God give me strength!" He heard his own unexpected words and wondered where they suddenly came from.

The blinding light struck again as Willie's fist came smashing in. The floor came up and jolted Tom's face. He didn't feel the floor when it hit him, though, as there was no feeling now—no feeling except a gripping desire inside him—like a fire, raging. He had to get up on his feet—he had to open his eyes and fight back. Finally, to his amazement, he could open his eyes just in time to duck Willie's savage kick with a hob-nailed boot. Willie's face was livid with a sort of grim pleasure. He had become a ferociously wild animal. Tom represented pampered privilege, something he had never known his entire life, so if Willie was going down, he wanted to completely destroy Tom Bristow.

Tom struggled to his feet and hung onto Willie's heavy arms for a moment. Suddenly he was in the midst of those grueling hours of hand-to-hand combat training during the weeks before he shipped out to Okinawa. Willie fully intended to kill him. Kill or be killed. Fear be damned!

Gathering all the strength he possessed, and with every ounce of rage and courage he could muster, Tom pushed himself away quickly from Willie's panting body and swung his fist into the loose, leering lips. Pain stabbed Tom's knuckles as they were gashed by the horsey teeth.

Willie's head snapped back. Shock flared in his eyes. The blow hurt Tom more than it did Willie, but it was worth it. Both men knew instantly that Willie was not invincible. Tom waded in, landing two more blows to the jaw.

Willie stormed forward roaring murderous oaths, brutal fists swinging wildly. Tom sidestepped deftly. The thunderous blows glanced off harmlessly. Willie stumbled and slammed to the floor. An exultant feeling of confidence swept through Tom and he knew that he could take Willie.

Willie struggled to his feet just as Tom spun and smashed his fist against the side of Willie's head. Willie lurched forward like a spent, bleeding toro, and Tom blasted him with all his strength squarely on the jaw.

Harriett, Sheriff Honeycutt and a gasping deputy ran into the room just as Willie's eyes went out of focus. The bully's heavy lips slackened into a sickly smirk, and he slid to the floor in a dismal, defeated, dispirited heap.

Dr. Paige Rongern had never been one to smile, as Tom remembered, but his slim features were unusually doleful now as he walked briskly into Benjamin's room. He was of medium build with a wild shock of steel-gray hair strewed carelessly over his head. The wild hair seemed out of place over the pleasant face. Dr. Rongern had been director of the Guymon Memorial Hospital since Tom's high school days and all of the region looked on him as their medical godfather.

Standing with Dr. Rongern was the neurosurgeon who had flown up from Amarillo, Dr. Phil Wilkins. Tom faced the two physicians, standing beside his father's hospital bed.

Thirty-six hours had passed since Benjamin was brought to the hospital. Thirty-hours ago Dr. Rongern had first introduced Tom to Dr. Wilkins.

"I can't say enough about what your son did in those first moments that mattered," Dr. Rongern began, speaking directly to the elder Bristow. "This young man did you a world of good through the initial dressing of the wound and for keeping you still before you were brought in. His cautious and expert handling probably saved you from complete paralysis."

"Complete paralysis?" Benjamin thundered. "What the hell are you getting at?" He looked away from Dr. Rongern to Dr. Wilkins, then finally to Tom, as though for reassurance. It was the first time in his entire lifetime Tom ever remembered his father looking at him that way.

Well," Dr. Rongern continued, "Dr. Wilkens here is as good as it gets when you want a top neurosurgeon."

"You know, Dr. Rongern—my boy here knows a lot about doctoring—he nearly—he just about—" He stopped and turned his head away from Tom and Dr. Rongern but Tom could see the brows knitting up and the mouth twisting in pain. He had managed to hide it almost altogether until now. "Get me off this damned bed, Dr. Rongern. My back's killing me. I just want to get to my ranch. I'll be okay there."

Dr. Rongern looked briefly at his medical colleague, then at the son, then directly at the father: "I'll be straightforward about this. Your back's going to take a long time to heal, if ever."

"And?" Benjamin asked, always one for the bottom line. "What does that mean?"

"It means," Dr. Rongern looked as if he would never get used to these life-changing moments, "there are some experimental techniques that Dr. Wilkins has pioneered. But without some kind of miracle, Mr. Bristow, you'll be a paraplegic the rest of your life."

The silence that followed was deafening, literally overwhelming. Then the father again looked at the son. His eyes begged for hope, for answers.

"Dad," Tom explained, "he's saying that you might be paralyzed from the waist down."

"I know what the hell a paraplegic is," Benjamin shot back, then his tone softened. "What are the chances for...?"

"Let me tell you what we know," Dr. Rongern continued. "Your respiratory problems have stabilized. There's no more fever. Traction will be increased. You'll get the best possible care right here for now." He looked over at Dr. Wilkins as though for confirmation.

"That's right, Mr. Bristow," Dr. Wilkins said. "Right now you're as well off here as any place you could be. When you stabilize, we will look toward flying you to Amarillo to operate and hopefully repair the damage to your spine. I have a colleague in New York City who knows more about this than anyone in the world. He has already agreed to fly in and help with the surgery when we are ready. Beyond that, I can't make any promises."

"There's no sense beating around the bush," Dr. Rongern added, looking at both Bristow men. "We're not out of the woods with this by any measure. You're looking at a long, hard road. Life is going to be different for you both. Real different."

He hesitated momentarily, looked in both men's eyes, then said, "But there's hope for both of you. Real hope. It's just going to take time."

Robert Boyd Delano

15

It had been one week to the day since the attack. The time passed quickly. Pastor Adam Taylor visited Benjamin's room daily, though he admittedly was making little progress in developing any kind of a relationship with the rancher. Still, he kept coming back.

Tom had spent as much time as possible at the hospital, yet he was also overseeing the remaining crew as they filled the new granaries with the wheat that had been piled, unprotected from the rain, on the dirt. The rains began falling soon after the crew completed the task.

Sunday morning, as the rains subsided, Tom decided to drive to the Elmhurst Cemetery, a short distance east of Guymon. It was the first time he had been able to get away to visit Anna's grave. He had visited the cemetery a number of times in the past, and he was surprised to see that the graves for Anna and Mrs. Taylor were only a stone's throw from his mother's final resting place.

He leaned over and touched Anna's freshly-chiseled name on the gravestone. The flower arrangements, so many in number, had wilted completely.

Tom sat on a bench next to Anna's grave for a half-hour, weeping and thinking about all the tender moments they had shared through the years. Then he took out the envelope Rev. Taylor had given him, taking care not to rip the flap as he opened it, and pulled the card out. There, in her unmistakably beautiful handwriting, were her last thoughts to him:

> My dearest Tom,
>
> Now you know why I said it was too late for us. I wish I could have told you about my illness, but once I knew there was no turning back for me, and once I had a peace about it, I couldn't bear to have you putting your life on hold for me. I cannot hold you back. You have so much to live for. Someday I know you will return to medicine, for it is your calling and destiny. You alone will know when the time is right for you to return.
>
> Don't be sad for me, my darling. I know where I am going, for I have based my life on God's promises. He has prepared a better place for me, and I will soon be graduating to my heavenly home. I am not afraid, but I am afraid for you.
>
> More than anything else right now, I want you to accept Jesus Christ into your heart and to grow to love Him as much as I do now. I cannot bear the thought of spending an eternity in heaven without you. Please read John 3:16

and Romans 1:12. Please make sure of your salvation through Jesus, God's only Son. Will you? For you? For me?

I love you with every breath I take. You were always the love of my life, and I will be waiting for you to meet me in heaven someday.

All my love,
Anna

"Did Anna ever let you read this note?" Tom asked the pastor as he walked into the Taylor home after the cemetary visit, holding the note at arm's length.

"No."

"Would you like to?"

"If you want me to read it."

Once they walked into the study, Anna's father read the note silently. Tears began falling down his leathery cheeks. When he was finished reading, he wiped away the tears and looked at Tom.

"My daughter was a rare soul," he began softly. "She truly understood God's purpose for her life. She knew why she was created. I have never met anyone who faced each responsibility as it arose with the talents God had given her. And she had the greatest gift of all, the ability to love both the lovely and the unlovely!"

Tom sat down in a leather chair, listening.

"You didn't know it, Tom, but my wife, the precious woman Anna cared for here all those years, was not her natural mother. The young girl who gave birth to Anna wasn't married. She came to the church one night, scared out of her mind, and begged Mrs. Taylor and me to look out for her little baby for a few days. We never heard from her after that. The authorities asked us if we would keep her for awhile. We had no children. We knew she was a priceless gift from God. And she was! She never gave us a single moment of trouble."

"She never told me," Tom mused. "What did she say when you told her?"

"She didn't say anything. We told her when she was six, when we thought she was old enough to understand. We told her how wonderful it was to be adopted, which is what we were in the process of doing then. We told her that God had adopted all of us into His family—all who accepted His Son as Savior. Anna just sat on the edge of Mrs. Taylor's bed and after a moment, she leaned over on Mrs. Taylor's shoulder and began crying. I don't think she was crying over her own lost mother, but she didn't say if she was. She cried for a little while and then stood up and smiled at Mrs. Taylor as if she were looking at her own flesh and blood. Then she wrapped her arms around my neck with the best hug I ever got in my whole life. That's just the kind of girl she was." Dr. Taylor wiped at his moist eyes with a handkerchief.

"Anna never mentioned it again," the parson continued when he regained his composure. "When my wife became ill, Anna took care of her just like she was… well…she was…"

The older man's voice broke and he paused again. After a moment he continued:

"She literally gave her life for her sick Mama. I used to marvel at Anna's patience, at her untiring efforts to comfort Mrs. Taylor. She never complained. She truly lived as if she were the hands and heart of God Himself down here on earth."

"She always made everyone feel special," Tom marveled. "I have never met anyone like her."

"We talked at length before she passed away," Rev. Taylor said. "This may sound strange, but I believe she was the happiest she had ever been. She truly looked upon going to heaven as a graduation."

Tom had leaned forward in his chair all the time the old minister was speaking, trying to grasp every word, trying to understand what he was saying. He measured the older minister's words against Higa, her yearning for "happy immortality," a yearning that was never fulfilled.

He thought about Benjamin, so desirous of respect and security, yet now he was paralyzed in a hospital bed with neither. He and his only son seemed to live in two totally different words with a chasm between.

He thought of Judge Anson and Jeanie. Their "live, love, laugh, and leave" philosophy hadn't seemed to bring lasting hope or happiness.

He thought of his own quest for love and meaning and freedom, yet he had never been able to reach anything that was remotely fulfilling. Every turn he had made had ended up running into a dead end.

The realization broke through. Of all the people I have ever known, Anna knew the truth. She knew the secret of immortality. Only it wasn't a secret at all.

"I still don't understand," Tom probed. "Anna had so many challenges. She gave her life for others, especially Mrs. Taylor. How could she be so happy all the time?"

"There is a verse in the Bible that she loved," Dr. Taylor replied softly. "It's found in Philippians 4:7."

The parson picked up a Bible sitting on his desk, turned the pages to the desired place, then he read: "And the peace of God, which passeth all understanding, shall keep your hearts and minds through Christ Jesus."

"I've never had that kind of peace," Tom admitted. "Never! I don't think I ever will."

Dr. Taylor laid the Bible down on his desk and looked

at Tom. He pointed to the Bible.

"The verse from Philippians was one of Anna's favorites," he said. "Let me share one of mine."

He folded his arms and looked past Tom, as though savoring the peace of the moment. The words came from his throat with dramatic sincerity as though each phrase was chiseled upon his heart: "O god of our salvation—who by thy strength—dost still the roaring of the seas, the roaring of their waves, the tumult of the peoples; thou makest the outgoings of the morning and the evening to shout for joy."

When he had finished, he looked at Tom and smiled, his finger tips resting gently on the Bible. What he had said reminded Tom of Higa's waka, yet so very different: Dr. Taylor spoke of things more eternal, more meaningful. The words seemed to be directly from God, resonating through the pastor.

"There's no reason why you or anyone else can't have the same peace and happiness that Anna had, and still has," Dr. Taylor continued. "God came to earth in the form of a man called Jesus, and He sacrificed His own earthly life to provide us with immortality. This is a gift that is ours for the asking while we are still here on earth."

"Why doesn't everyone ask for it then?" Tom asked.

"Good question. It's because most of us want to do everything for ourselves so we can glorify our own achievements. Only those like Anna learn the peace and joy and power and immortality that come from God alone. He can give us the ability to do whatever task comes before us, no matter how small or how great. Just read this Book and you will know the truth. That truth will set you free, Tom."

"The truth will set you free!"

The words were like shafts of light piercing Tom's heart. This was the freedom for which he had been searching for so long. Anna had told him the same phrase several times, but somehow it had never made sense to him before. Now the pieces all slipped into place in a meaningful pattern.

Tom walked to the window and looked out. There was lots of space out there—lots of freedom—but it was inside, inside his own heart, where he wanted freedom most desperately.

He struggled to maintain his composure. Suddenly he wanted to bolt for the door.

"I've got to go!"

"Are you sure?"

"Yes," Tom said firmly. "I've got to go."

"Here," Dr. Taylor said, walking up beside Tom and holding a small Bible out to him. "Take this. It contains all the truth and wisdom you'll ever need."

Tom took the Bible, running his hands over the rough black cover.

"Thank you," the younger man said, struggling with his thoughts. "This Bible looks just like one Anna gave me a long time ago when I was shipping out to the Pacific."

"It is the Bible Anna gave you then." Dr. Taylor smiled. "You told her you wanted to leave it with her for safekeeping. Anna kept it with her things. She prayed you would someday come back for it. That you would be ready for the truth in this book."

Tom felt a cold chill run through his veins.

"I'm going to read it this time," he said, "for Anna."

Dr. Taylor's face beamed and he put his hand on Tom's shoulder as they walked together out to the front porch.

"I've got a better idea, Tom. Do it for yourself."

They stood there in the mid-day brightness saying nothing for a moment. Tom glanced about at the empty swing and the floor beneath, worn slick from Anna's feet. He looked at the neatly trimmed grass, and finally at Dr. Taylor himself, at his warm blue eyes, deep in wisdom, with a touch of merriment.

At that moment he felt such a connection and love for this man who had nurtured such good things in Anna.

Dr. Taylor's hand-shake was firm and strong. "I wish you would stay, Tom. But I'm always as close as the phone. Feel free to stop by anytime."

All Tom could manage to say was "Thank you." He wanted to say more but the words seemed to gather around the lump lodged in his throat.

Tom sat on the windmill ledge, looking over the vast expanse of the Hawk Ranch. To the east, he could see field after field of wheat stubble. To the north he could see past Goff Creek and all the way to Kansas. To the west he could see immense pasture lands, dotted in places with purebred Hereford and Angus cattle. To the south, he could see Guymon on the horizon, the place where his father's unfeeling body rested and healed from the beating he had taken. Beyond Guymon was the Elmhurst Cemetery, the final resting place for Anna, Mrs. Taylor, and his own mother.

Sure that no one around the ranch could see what he was doing, he opened the Bible Anna had given him so long ago.

"I didn't need You then," he began praying to a God he wasn't sure even existed, "but if You are there, I sure need You now."

He opened Anna's hand-written note, looked for the Scripture verses she had suggested, then looked in the Bible's Table of Contents to see where those two books of the Bible were located.

"For God so loved the world," he read out loud from John 3:16, "that he gave his only begotten Son, that whosoever believeth in him should not perish, but have everlasting life."

Everlasting life!
Immortality!

Then he turned to the other verse Anna wanted him to read, John 12:1—"But as many as received him, to them gave he power to become the sons of God, even to them that believe on his name:"

Receive Him?
Believe on His name?

Then Tom saw Anna's note beside that verse. As if she were leaving clues to a secret treasure, she had written "Revelation 3:20."

Even Tom knew that it was the final book in the Bible. He turned there and began reading: "Behold, I stand at the door, and knock: if any man hear my voice, and open the door, I will come in to him, and will sup with him, and he with me."

This didn't seem like such a secret after all. It was right there in the Bible, open to anyone who chose to read the words.

Tom watched a hawk fly over the ranch house. His past, present and future seemed to be crossing paths at that precise moment.

"Lord Jesus, I...I..." he stumbled to say the right words. Finally the words broke like a rushing stream pouring directly from a breaking heart. "I've made a mess of my life. I tried to do it all on my own. I've made so many bad decisions. Now, like Anna tried to get me to do so many times, I'm asking You to come into my heart. Take away all the horrible stuff. I want eternal life, just like You promised. And I need you to help me... to help me..."

The hawk continued circling overhead. A slight breeze drifted past. And for the first time in a long time, Tom was a child once more, sitting in his own private, lofty haven.

Free!

16

Benjamin lay with his face to the wall. Tom could see that his father's eyes were open. One arm moved ever so slightly as the younger man entered the Amarillo hospital room. It was one month, to the day, since the initial conversation back in Guymon with Dr. Rongern and Dr. Wilkins. So much had happened. Now the long-awaited spinal surgery was over. The doctors, especially Dr. Grover who had flown in from New York City, seemed cautiously pleased.

The lights were dimmed, almost completely dark, in Benjamin's recovery room. A small window let in just enough of the evening light to cast vague shadows through the room.

"Dad?"

Tom's voice echoed off the walls as though he were in an empty tomb. Benjamin didn't move or answer.

"Dad?"

Tom said louder. He sat down on the edge of the bed and put his hand on the old man's arm. It was like a seasoned stick of wood.

Then the old rancher's head turned toward him, his eyes glistening. He opened his mouth to speak, the thin throat working, but unable to voice any words. He pulled an arm out from under the sheet and grabbed Tom around the shoulder, pulling him down against his boney chest, holding his son tightly. Tom felt as though he was caught in a vice, and he sensed his father was holding him that way so Tom couldn't see the tears in his own eyes. He could feel the old man's chest shudder with sobs and the powerful, proud heart thumping like a bounding coyote after a rabbit.

Tom lay there in his father's grip a long time—until after the light from the window had faded away and left them in almost complete darkness. Neither one said anything. The chasm had been bridged and a well-worn bridge it would be. Its foot boards would be worn smooth like the ones between Anna and her mother, the ones Anna had walked over so many times.

Benjamin had needed him during the past weeks as never before. Tom had risen to the task. Not only had he overseen the Bristow farming and ranching operations admirably, but he had become more and more aware that someday, when his father was better, he would… he must…return to medicine. Too much had happened for him to do anything else.

Talks with Pastor Taylor had helped. He had been devouring the Bible Anna had given him.

He realized, beyond any shadow of doubt, that God had placed the gift of medicine deep inside him. As he grew in the knowledge of God's will and direction, he knew that gift was undeniably linked to learning more about the true secret of being a happy, joyful, fulfilled immortal. For the first time, all the pieces of his life were beginning to fit together.

Right now, though, his father needed him. It was anything but easy. The old man could be a cross, cranky curmudgeon at times. Both of them knew that it might be months, years—if ever—before Benjamin could walk again. Some things might never change. But the bridge between father and son had been repaired, even as it had weathered the mightiest of challenges.

Tom reached over in the darkness and felt for his father's hand. He found and grasped it. The hand, much like the old rancher himself, was rough and calloused and unbending.

Tom held it firmly. Lovingly.